When I got into my room there was somebody in my bed, all right, and it wasn't anyone I would want to chase away.

It was Melody Gilman, and she smiled shyly as I lit the lamp and looked at her.

"How'd you get in?" I asked.

"The back door."

"What about your father?"

"He had to go out of town to deliver a baby," she said. "He'll most likely be gone until tomorrow. Are you glad to see me?"

I was and I wasn't, but I told her I was. Maybe she sensed my reserve, because she lowered the blanket to show me that she was totally and invitingly naked.

She didn't have to ask me again if I was glad to see her.

Don't miss any of the lusty, hard-riding action in the
new Charter Western series, THE GUNSMITH:

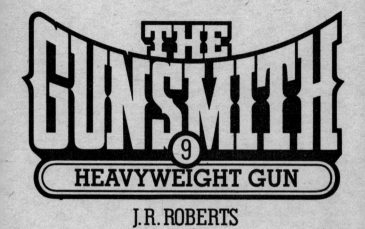

THE GUNSMITH

9

HEAVYWEIGHT GUN

J.R. ROBERTS

CHARTER BOOKS, NEW YORK

THE GUNSMITH #9: HEAVYWEIGHT GUN

A Charter Book / published by arrangement with
the author

PRINTING HISTORY
Charter original / September 1982
Second printing / March 1983
Third printing / April 1984

ISBN: 0-441-30923-2

Charter Books are published by The Berkley Publishing Group,
200 Madison Avenue, New York, New York 10016.
PRINTED IN THE UNITED STATES OF AMERICA

Prologue
Willow Falls, Arizona
1873

Young Bat Masterson was beginning to regret having decided to start his career as a fight promoter in the town of Willow Falls, Arizona. The way things were shaping up, there was likely to be more fighting outside of the ring than inside of it. Most of that would be done by the Currys, and probably among themselves. And then there was the fiery Maggie Harris, a lovely brunette whose sole aim in life seemed to be to make her younger brother, Billy, heavyweight champion of the world. Bat thought that was a waste of a good woman, but he was too busy to try and change her mind. He had the fights to promote, and a lovely little thing he was trying his best to keep happy as it was. No, he had no free time to try and change Maggie Harris's mind about anything.

Although the Currys—Dan and his three sons, Dave, Dell and Don—fought among themselves constantly, they pulled together when it came to one thing, and that was making Don, the youngest of them, heavyweight champion of the world. For this reason, they clashed often with Maggie Harris, who did her best to keep Billy away from Don Curry, until they could meet in the ring.

There were other fighters in Bat's tournament, but to everyone's way of thinking, when it came down to the final two, it would be young Billy Harris against young Don Curry.

Neither fighter was a local; they had come to Willow Falls to attend the tournament, the winner of which would face heavyweight champ Mike McCoole, who was touring the West and taking on all comers.

Bat was lying in the bed of Bonnie Mapes, who was sleeping peacefully by his side, and he was hoping that the profits from this tournament would be worth all of the trouble he was having to put up with.

He looked over at Bonnie, who was lying on her back with her hair covering her face. He reached over and brushed back her golden hair so that he could see her face clearly. She was only nineteen, a year younger than he, and they had met when she waited on him in the café. There had been a strong mutual attraction and it hadn't taken long before he was sharing her bed.

She was a little thing, barely five feet tall, with long blond hair, wide blue eyes, a full-lipped, rosebud mouth and smooth, full, creamy breasts topped by large, pink nipples. She was energetic in bed and more uninhibited and inventive than any young girl he had run across before.

She had been a constant delight to him over the

past two weeks, as he struggled to get the tournament going, and to keep the cocky young fighters away from each other until they were inside the ring. Now that he was ready to get the first elimination fight underway, things had started to go wrong. Three fighters had had disabling accidents, and he had the distinct, troubling impression that these had in fact been carefully planned incidents, meant to cut down on the competition.

If he were right, that still didn't tell him who was behind them. Could Maggie Harris want the championship for her brother so much? Didn't she have enough confidence in his ability to win the title in the ring? And what about old man Dan Curry? With the help of his boys he could easily cut down the number of competitors that Don would have to face.

Or was it someone else entirely?

Bat had sunk too much money into this tournament to stand by now and watch it all go to waste. He needed help, but there wasn't anyone in town he could trust enough to ask. He was almost sorry he had split up with his friend Wyatt Earp, but Wyatt was still chasing his dream of opening a large gambling hall, while Bat had decided to try something different. You couldn't find a gun like Wyatt's to back you up just anywhere. They didn't just come riding down the main street of town. . . .

Sunlight was streaming through the window when he threw back the sheets and got out of bed without disturbing Bonnie. They had given each other quite a workout last night, and he could feel the effects in his legs.

He walked to the window and, squinting at the brightness, pulled back the curtain to peer out.

Son of a bitch! He couldn't believe his eyes as he looked down upon the main street. There, riding into town, was a gun that could not only rival Wyatt Earp's, but probably even surpass it.

He hurriedly dressed, waking Bonnie in his haste.

"What's the rush, Bat?" she asked, sleepily. She sat up, allowing the sheet to drop away from her luscious breasts. Bat couldn't control the stirring he felt in his loins, and he stopped with one leg still outside his pants.

"There's someone riding into town who could take a lot of weight off my shoulders just about now," he explained.

"Who is he?"

"An old friend."

"A good friend?" she asked.

"A very good friend," he answered.

"Oh," she said. She kicked with her legs, dropping the coverlets to the floor. Totally naked now, she preened for Bat, bending her legs at the knees and arching her back slightly to display her ample chest.

"Good enough to take you away from this?"

He dropped his pants to the floor and kicked them away, then proceeded to remove his undergarments.

"Nobody is that good a friend, Bonnie," he told her, joining her on the bed.

The man who was riding into town was a good enough friend—and a good enough gun—that Bat felt he had cause to celebrate. And right then he couldn't think of a better way than getting back into bed with Bonnie Mapes.

It looked as if the tournament might be a success after all.

ONE

Willow Falls, Arizona appeared to be a sleepy, moderately sized town, but appearances had deceived me before, so I reserved judgment as I guided my team down the main street of the town.

Had I known that Bat Masterson was already there, I might have decided to bypass it all together. Not that I didn't like Bat. That wasn't the case at all. The last time I had seen him, though, he and Wyatt Earp and I had almost gotten ourselves killed, and it had been my experience rather than their youthful enthusiasm that had probably prevented it from happening. To Bat's credit, however, his youthful zeal was tempered by intelligence and skill.

Anyway, in looking back, I could have stayed out of that fracas with Bat and Wyatt, but it always seemed that if I had a fifty-fifty chance of avoiding trouble, I usually ended up walking right into the thick of it.

This time was no different.

I located the livery and put up my team, rig and Duke. Then I took my saddlebags and went in

1

search of a hotel. On the way, I passed a saloon—that is, I started to pass a saloon, but my overwhelming thirst prevailed upon me to stop in for a cold beer.

Behind the bar was a sign announcing a boxing tournament being held in town, which was to start in two days.

"What's that all about?" I asked the bartender as he set my beer down in front of me.

"Ain't you heard? Mike McCoole, the heavyweight champ of the world is touring the West, taking on all comers. This is to be his last stop. There's them that think that Willow Falls is the place to catch him and take his title away."

"If he still has it when he gets here," I commented.

"He will," the man said, sounding sure. He looked himself like an ex-fighter, though he was only about five-seven or so. "I've seen Mike McCoole in action, friend, and no tougher man ever stepped into a ring."

"You look like you've been in a ring yourself a few times," I said.

"I was a fair man with my fists in my time."

"You ever fight McCoole?"

"I wasn't in his class," the barkeep admitted. "My name's Ben Neal. Iron Ben Neal, they used to call me."

"Why is that?"

"I was never put down in one hundred and three fights," he explained, and his face carried the evidence that he had absorbed a lot of punishment during his ring career.

"How many of those fights did you win?" I asked.

"I lost more than I won," he said, "but no man ever put me down. If I had been a little fancier—well, no sense in looking back now."

"Is there anyone in town you think might give McCoole a run for his money?" I asked, getting interested. If there were to be some decent fights held, I wouldn't mind sticking around to watch.

"None of the local boys, but there's a couple of out-of-town lads who might give him a go. Only one will get a shot at him, though. That's what the tournament is all about, picking out the man who'll face McCoole when he gets here."

"And when will that be?"

"A week, maybe two."

That was a long time to hang around on the chance that there might be a decent fight in the offing.

"You wondering if it's worth sticking around?" Neal asked.

"What do you think?"

He shrugged. "If you ain't going nowhere in a hurry, it might be interesting," he said.

"How about another beer while I think it over?"

"Comin' up."

I watched him fetch my beer while I thought it over. He was about forty-four or five, and he moved kind of stiff, as if he had a bad leg.

Was I going anywhere in a hurry? I'd begun to think about that more and more lately. Where was I going? Where had I gone and what had I accomplished since giving up my badge almost three years ago?

I guess a man starts to think about that when he gets to be forty-one, and I was getting pretty close. Even without the badge, I hadn't been able to stay away from trouble and gunplay. Maybe I needed to stay in one place for a while and think things over.

He brought my second beer and said, "What'd you decide, friend?"

"I might stay around a while," I answered, "on your recommendation."

"What's your name?"

"Adams, Clint Adams."

I watched him closely to see if he recognized the name. If he had, I might have moved on right there and then, but he didn't show any sign at all of having heard of me. Maybe if I had been a famous boxer . . .

"Pleased to meet you, Mr. Adams," he said, extending his hand. He had a firm grip, and I could see the muscles in his forearms and biceps as we shook hands.

"Call me Clint," I said.

"And you can call me Ben," he replied. "You can pay me for the first beer, but the second one's on the house."

"Much obliged," I said, flipping a coin onto the bar. "Where's the best place in town to get a room?"

"Hotel right down the block," he said. "Tell 'em I sent you over."

"Much obliged again."

"You might meet the young feller who's promotin' this boxing tournament," he said. "He's got hisself a room in the hotel."

"Young fella?" I asked.

"Can't be more than twenty or so. I hear he's got hisself a reputation with a gun in some parts."

"Is that so?" I asked. "What might his name be?"

He thought a moment, then said, "Bat something or other. Funny name, ain't it?"

"Bat Masterson?"

"That's it, that's the feller. You know him?"

"I know him," I said. "Thanks for all the information."

"You're welcome, Clint. I hope something happens to make your stay worthwhile."

Something happened, all right, but whether it made my stay worthwhile or not was another matter entirely.

TWO

I went over to the hotel and got a room facing the street. I mentioned Ben Neal's name, but I don't know that it got me any special treatment. I still had to pay for one night, in advance.

I had just removed my boots and stretched out on the bed when there was a knock on the door.

"Come on in, Bat," I called.

Bat walked in with a puzzled frown on his face.

"Now how the hell did you know it was me?" he asked, closing the door behind him. He still looked the same, a handsome youngster who liked to get duded up. When you dress the way he does, you have to be tough—and he was. I'd seen evidence of that in the past.

"I heard about your boxing tournament," I explained. "I was told that it was being run by some young fella with a funny first name. The rest was just an educated guess."

"Guess, hell," he said, approaching the bed. I sat up and we shook hands. He was half my age, but there were few men I would rather have backing my play.

6

I knew he felt the same, and I knew he was going to ask me to back his. Bat had never had any difficulty finding trouble, and once he found it he met it head on.

"Pull up a chair and tell me about your action," I invited him.

He showed me the bottle of whiskey he was holding in his right hand and said, "No glasses, but we've roughed it before, right?"

I reached for it and said, "Right."

While I uncorked the bottle he pulled a chair over and sat down. He briefly ran down the idea behind the tournament. Entry fees and low overhead gave him a high rate of profit.

"What about the fighter's purses?" I asked.

"Mike McCoole is all the purse they want," he said, taking the bottle back and pulling on it.

"Sounds like a sweet deal," I commented, "unless McCoole shows up without the title, or doesn't show up at all."

He made a face, but admitted, "Those are possible eventualities, but not my immediate problem."

"Oh? You have a problem?"

"A few of the fighters have had accidents."

"What kind of accidents?"

"The kind that will keep them from fighting."

"Any fatal?"

"Not yet."

I thought it over a moment, then said, "Yeah, I guess you've got some problems, all right."

"I could use a hand, Clint . . . for a piece of the action, of course."

"All right," I said.

"Of course, I'll have to take the largest share," he went on, "but I'll give you a fair share of—wait a minute." He had finally realized that I didn't appear to need convincing. "What did you say?"

"I said, all right. I'll help you."

"Without hearing the split?"

"The split will be fair," I said.

He handed me back the bottle and said, "You had already decided to back me, didn't you?"

"Yep."

"How'd you know I had trouble?" he asked.

"You and trouble go hand in hand, Bat."

I gave him back the bottle and stood up.

"You want to fill me in on what we're dealing with here?" I asked.

"The whole tournament looks like it will boil down to two men."

"That's what Ben Neal told me."

"You talk to Neal? Sure, you would have stopped in the saloon right off. Ben knows fighting, and he thinks the same way."

"Any accidents happen to these two?"

He shook his head and said, "No."

"That doesn't make sense. If somebody was looking to rig this thing, those two would be the first targets."

"That's what I figured," he said. "I can't explain it."

"Fill me in on those two first, and then give me the rest," I suggested.

"Billy Harris is a kid from the East," he began. "His sister brought him here because she figures that this is the place to catch McCoole when he's ready to be taken. Her brother is twenty-two, McCoole is about thirty-five. She figures at the end of the tour, McCoole will be set up for her brother."

"The kid is good?" I asked.

"He's got good hands, Clint, and his sister's got a sharp tongue. She's a looker, but she's a hellcat."

"How confident is she?"

"She seems pretty damned sure of her little brother, but I guess a few accidents wouldn't hurt his chances."

"Who is the other fighter?"

"His name's Curry, Don—"

"Kin to Dan Curry?" I asked.

"His youngest boy. You know Curry?"

"Is Dell here, too?" I asked, getting a cold feeling in my gut.

"He's here," Bat said. "Where do you know the Currys from?"

"I know Dan and Dell," I answered, "and I knew the oldest boy, Dan, Jr."

"I didn't know there was a Dan, Jr." Bat said.

"There isn't, anymore," I said. "I killed him a dozen years ago."

"Oh, I see."

"I was supposed to bring him in, and he drew on me. He left me no choice."

"I guess they won't feel too friendly towards you when they find out you're in town. If you want to change your mind—"

"I'll stick around," I assured him.

"What about Dave and Don? Will they know you?"

"By name I'm sure, but not by sight. They were too young."

"Dell is supposed to be the mean one, isn't he?"

"He's mean, and he can handle a gun. You haven't had any run-ins with him yet, have you?"

"Nothing major. I've been trying to keep them and Maggie Harris off each other's throat. That Dell, though, I think he's got his eye on more than just her throat."

"He would."

Dell fancied himself a ladies' man, and in some parts I guess he was.

"What does she think of him?"

"She's got a one-track mind, Clint. She wants her brother to be champ."

"She must be decent looking to interest Dell."

"She's more than decent," Bat said, "but she doesn't seem to be interested in men, except for her brother's opponents, and Mike McCoole." Shaking his head he said, "She's obsessed with beating him. If she could get into the ring and do it herself, I think she would."

"Personal?" I asked. "Does she know him?"

He shrugged. "Beats me. Not that I know of, but I haven't gotten real close to the lady."

"Not interested?" I asked.

He smiled and said, "I like to take them one at a time, Clint."

"I don't blame you. Are the Currys staying in town?"

He shook his head.

"They've taken over an abandoned ranch house outside of town. They're using it as a training camp."

"And the Harris girl and her brother?"

"They're in town, at the boarding house down the street. They're using the corral behind the livery to train in."

"Okay. Before you run the rest of them down for me, let's get straight just what it is you want me to do."

"I've got to concentrate on getting this thing off right, and on time. I want you to try and make sure there are no more accidents. If there is one, I hope you'll be able to catch whoever caused it."

"I'm security, then."

"Right."

I looked out the window at the quiet street, then turned and walked back to the bed.

"Pass me that bottle and let's go over everyone involved, even the fighters who have already had accidents. I have to have some idea of who I'm dealing with."

I listened with half an ear, though, because I already knew more than I wanted to when I found out the Currys were in town.

THREE

All of the other fighters in the tournament seemed to be more or less local boys. Maggie and Billy Harris were from the East somewhere, and I knew that the Currys were from Oklahoma way. The others all seemed to be from somewhere in Arizona, if not Willow Falls itself.

Bat and I agreed that I should be presented to the competitors and their "managers" as the co-promoter of the tournament. I agreed to use my real name, which Bat thought some might recognize, putting an instant stop to anymore accidents. Besides, two of the Currys already knew me, so there was really no chance of hiding my true identity.

After Bat had run down the local fighters for me, we agreed to meet in the café for lunch, after I took a bath and changed into some clean clothes. When he left, I did some thinking about him. He was twenty years old or so, and where was he headed? He seemed to be most interested in gambling, women and guns, not necessarily in that order. I thought that perhaps sometime during the next week I might talk to him and see if I couldn't help give his life some direction. I didn't want him to find himself wondering what his life was like when he turned forty. By then a man should know, or he had more than likely wasted most of it.

Or maybe I should just keep my nose out from where it didn't belong. I went downstairs and asked the clerk if the hotel had bathing facilities. For two-bits I got a hot bath, then changed into some fresh clothes and went out to check the town out before meeting Bat for lunch.

It was a small town, but it had all of the necessities. There was the saloon, two hotels, a boarding house, a cathouse that also served as a saloon, a church, a livery stable and all of the stores a growing town needed. I didn't know if the town was growing or not, but if heavyweight champion Mike McCoole came here and lost his title, the town might very well do some serious growing whether it wanted to or not.

I stopped into the livery to check on Duke, who had been well taken care of, and while there I heard some commotion going on out back. I went out that way and saw two men circling each other in the middle of the corral. One of them was a tall youngster who looked as if he were chiseled out of stone. He had huge biceps, muscular legs and a chest that look like two cement slabs. The other man was older and not in as good shape. He was virtually defenseless against the attack of the younger man, and while I watched he was easily pummeled to the ground.

That was when I first saw Maggie Harris.

"Damn it," she shouted, hopping off the fence where she had been seated, "I paid you to give him a workout, three rounds at least, and you go and get yourself knocked out in the first thirty seconds?"

As she berated the fallen man, he could barely hear her. He was shaking his head in a vain attempt to clear it, and then she turned her back on him and I saw her face.

She had long, dark hair and wide brown eyes that were now flaming with anger and frustration. Her nostrils were flaring as she fumed, and her full lips were compressed together. She had large, full breasts and a small waist, and her legs appeared to be incredibly long. In the pants and boots she was wearing, she looked nearly six feet tall, but she was still dwarfed by "little" brother, who appeared to be about six-four or five.

"If we can't get you a decent sparring partner in this jerkwater town, how the hell are we going to get you in shape?"

I backed away and went into the livery again, because Billy Harris looked like he was in pretty good shape to me, and I wanted to go and meet Bat before she spotted me and tried to get *me* to go three rounds with him.

To say the least, both of the Harrises were pretty impressive.

FOUR

I went to the café and found Bat already waiting for me.

"Where've you been?" he asked.

"I went over to check on my horse," I answered, and then went on to explain that I had seen Billy Harris working out.

"Did you see Maggie?" Bat asked.

"I did, and I was impressed. She has a fine figure, and a sharp tongue."

"Right on both counts. You don't know how sharp a tongue until it's been aimed at you."

"That's something I'm hoping to avoid," I said. "Have you ordered lunch?"

Bat shook his head and said, "I waited for you."

So we both ordered and then started talking about the Harrises again.

"Talking about fine figures," I said, "young Billy isn't built so bad, either. What's the Curry kid look like?"

"He's big, as big as Billy, but thicker around the middle. He's probably stronger, but Billy's faster."

"And nobody else looks like they have a chance?"

"Naw," he said shaking his head, "It'll come down to those two, sure as shootin'."

"That would make the Harrises and the Currys our prime suspects, then, as far as the accidents are concerned."

"I guess, although I can't understand why either of them would think it was necessary."

"I suppose that's what I'm here to find out, right?"

"Right."

After lunch we decided to have Bat introduce me to both Maggie and Billy Harris. I still hadn't decided how I was going to handle the Currys, and it was better to avoid them until I did decide.

We went over to the livery to see if he was still working out, and he was. Another man was sparring with him, but this one didn't seem to be faring any better.

"Ooh," Bat said, flinching as Billy Harris landed a right to the body that caused his sparring partner to sink slowly to the ground.

"Ouch," I said, just to say something.

"Damn!" Maggie Harris said.

"I'm sorry," Billy Harris said with his hands spread wide, and I didn't know if he was apologizing to the man he'd knocked down, or his sister.

"Why can't we find any decent sparring partners in this town?" Maggie Harris demanded to know, looking skyward.

Bat climbed into the corral and he and Billy helped the fallen man to his feet.

"I'm sorry, mister," Billy told him.

The man nodded, holding his side, and staggered over to Maggie Harris.

"You're stealing my money," she told him, handing him ten dollars.

That didn't seem to bother him as much as his side did. He took the money, stuffed it into his pocket, and then walked off hugging himself with both arms.

"Masterson!" Maggie Harris called out.

"Yes, Maggie," Bat said in a resigned tone.

"You've got to get me some decent sparring partners for Billy. How can we expect to be ready for Don Curry?"

"Maggie, I suspect that Curry is having the same problem," Bat reasoned.

"That's bull. He's got brothers as big as him, he's probably using them to spar with."

Bat looked at me and I looked at the sky, because she had a valid point there. Don Curry could have sparred with his old man and gotten a workout from it.

"You looking to make some money, friend?" I heard her ask. When I looked at her I saw that she was talking to me.

"Uh, all the time—but not that way," I answered, pointing to her brother.

"Why not? You look like you could handle yourself." She was trying to shame me into it, and I decided to fight back.

"With you, maybe," I said, "but not with him."

For an aggressive woman, she didn't know how to handle that.

"Bat?" she said, turning away from me.

"Maggie, I'll try to come up with somebody for you," he said, walking over to us. "Why don't you give the kid a break?"

She stared at Bat for a moment, hands on hips, then turned at the waist and called to her brother, "Go get cleaned up, Billy."

"Sure, sis," he replied, and he went off to obey.

"Maggie, I want you to meet Clint Adams," Bat said to Maggie Harris. She turned her head towards me and regarded me critically. "Clint is a friend of mine and he's agreed to co-promote the fights with me. Clint, this is Maggie Harris. Her brother Billy is the fighter, and Maggie's the trainer and manager—and probably the brains."

"Billy's bright enough," she said to Bat while looking at me, "he just needs to be told what to do once in a while." She hesitated a moment, then surprised me by sticking out her hand for me to shake.

"Your name sounds familiar to me, Mr. Adams," she said as we shook hands.

"Does it?"

"I've heard it, or seen it somewhere before."

"You're from the East, aren't you?" I asked her.

"That's right. Why?"

"No reason in particular," I said. I wondered if she had seen or heard my name since coming West, or while she was back East. Had my name traveled that far?

"Don't tell me, Mr. Adams," she went on, "it'll come to me."

"Well, while you're waiting for it to hit you, why don't you call me Clint?"

"Fine, and you can call me Maggie. We'll have to talk later, Clint. I'm curious as to what you think you can bring to these contests that would make you want to be co-promoter."

"You name the time and place, Maggie, and we'll talk," I agreed.

"I'll let you know," she promised. "Bat, get me some sparring partners that won't fall down everytime Billy breathes on them, all right?"

"I'll try, Maggie."

She accepted that and went off to find her brother. We both watched her walk until she disappeared into the stable. She was wearing pants, and filled them out from behind very nicely. She was a big girl.

"Good-looking woman," Bat remarked.

"Can't argue that."

"Tough, too, but I think she liked you," he said.

I gave him a sideways look and said, "I'll let you know."

FIVE

The remainder of the day was spent getting me introduced to most of the other participants, and we finished up the day at the saloon.

"Any chance of a game?" I asked.

"Might find a few guys willing to play you," he said. "I seem to have worn out my welcome at poker in this town."

"I hope it was worth it to you."

Iron Ben Neal was behind the bar, and he set up two beers for us.

"Ben, you've met Clint."

"I have."

"Clint's going to co-promote the tournament with me. We're old friends."

"I hope we can call on you, Ben, if we need any professional help," I said.

Iron Ben's chest swelled as he said, "You sure can, Clint. Anything I can do to help, you just let me know."

"I will, Ben. Thanks."

We picked up our beers and walked to an empty corner table.

"What was that for?" Bat asked.

I shrugged.

"You never know, we might need him."

"I guess—if we ever have to teach the fighters to catch punches with their faces."

Bat took the first chair while I walked around the table to sit with my back to the wall. Sitting that way was a consequence of the life I'd been forced to lead. Bat had five or six years of living the way he did before he would also be forced into never sitting with his back to the door.

"Bat, have you ever thought about settling down?" I asked.

"What, you mean get married?" he asked in disbelief.

"Not necessarily. Just settling down to one place, one town, and living a normal life."

"What's normal for some people ain't necessarily normal for others. Clint. You should know that. You've lived in one place for long periods of time. What are you doing now?"

"Drifting," I admitted.

"Right. Maybe I'll do it the other way around. I'll drift a while, and then maybe I'll settle down," he said. Then he thought a moment and added, "Maybe," again.

He drank some beer and said, "What do you want to do, convert me?"

"No," I replied, "forget it."

He frowned at me, but took me at my word and forgot about it.

We talked some about the fighters, and then got onto the subject of the Currys.

"How are they going to react to your being in town?" he asked me.

"We'll find that out sooner or later. I never knew a Curry who could stay away from a saloon for very long."

"Is that why we're here, so you can wait for them?" he asked. "Isn't that asking for trouble?"

"I've got to come face to face with one or all of them sooner or later, Bat. I might as well pick the time and place."

"I guess you're right."

"Why don't you go and do whatever you've got to do," I suggested.

"I've got nothing special on for tonight," he said. "At least, not until later on tonight. I'll stick around for a while."

"Suit yourself."

"I usually do."

Brash and cocky, that was Bat Masterson. It came with youth, but it would wear off, sooner or later. Then he'd either get careful or bitter—or dead.

"You see anybody in here who might like a game?" I asked him.

He looked around the room. "Some, but now that they've seen you sitting with me, I doubt that they'll sit down with you." He leaned forward and added, "They'd probably think I gave you lessons on how to play poker."

"You?" I said. "You couldn't give me lessons in solitaire, let alone poker."

"Is that so?"

"You know it."

"Well, why don't we get a deck of cards and—what's the matter?" he asked, noticing the change that had come over my face.

"Curry," I said, looking at the front door.

"Which one?" he asked, starting to turn.

"All of them."

He turned and saw what I saw: Dan Curry and his three sons—Dave, Dell and young Don.

"Jesus," I whispered, looking at the face of the younger boy.

"What?"

"He looks just like his brother."

"Which brother?"

"Dan, Jr.," I said. "The one I killed."

Don was the spitting image of his older brother, who had forced me to kill him twelve years before. Don would only have been about eight then, and Dave about ten. That made the youngest Curry twenty and Dave twenty-two. Dell, the oldest living brother, was about thirty-five now, two years younger than his older brother would have been.

The old man had aged badly. Once he had been a physically imposing man, but he had lost a lot of weight during the twelve years since I'd last seen him, and he was a shadow of the powerful man he once was. He still had his height, six-three at least, but his once broad and well-padded shoulders were now slumped and bony.

His boys were another story, though. They were all tall and powerfully built, especially Don. He was a monster, just like his older brother had been. He was taller than Billy Harris, and heavier in the shoulders as well as through the middle.

"Billy Harris will have to be fast to last with that kid," I said.

"He is," Bat assured me. "He's fast enough to stay with him, but I don't know if he can take him."

"He doesn't wear a gun," I pointed out.

"The other three do, though," Bat added.

Apparently Dell or the old man didn't see me. I doubted that the other two would have recognized me even if they had seen me.

"Uh-oh," Bat said as they all walked to the bar.

"What's the matter?"

"Iron Ben," he said. "He's got a big mouth, as you know. He's bound to tell them about the new co-promoter."

"They'd find out one way or another, Bat," I said.

"You say the older one will remember you?"

"Without a doubt. He was about twenty-three then."

"He's pretty good with a gun, I hear."

"He wasn't then, but I've heard the same."

"He may slap leather as soon as he turns around."

"I doubt it."

Bat looked at me, puzzled.

"The old man's wasted away some, but I'd be willing to bet that none of those boys wipes his nose without the old man telling him to. I'll have to deal with old Dan, first."

"He looks like a good stiff breeze would knock him over," Bat observed.

"He used to be built like an oak tree," I said,

"just like his boys. Something must have happened to him."

"Yeah, he got old."

"We all get old, Bat," I said. I put both of my hands on the table and left them there.

"There he goes," Bat said, as we watched Iron Ben start talking. Suddenly, the old man's spine went ramrod straight and I knew he had just heard my name.

"Here it comes," I warned Bat. He pushed his chair back so he'd be able to get at his gun easier. "Go easy, Bat."

Dell Curry turned around real quick and searched the room, his eyes flicking jerkily about. When he spotted me it was only the old man's frail hand that kept him from rushing across the room at me. The other two boys also turned around, but they were looking a bit puzzled.

The old man spoke to them, and then he and his oldest son walked towards Bat and me, leaving the other two at the bar.

"Masterson," old Dan greeted as they reached our table. The look of hatred in Dell Curry's eyes made his face the ugliest I'd ever seen.

"Mr. Curry," Bat replied.

"Why is this man involved with the tournament?" Dan asked.

"He's my partner, Mr. Curry," Bat told him. "That's all you have to know."

"Then I'll tell you all you need to know, Masterson," Dan Curry said. He pointed a long, bony finger at me and said, "This man killed my oldest son twelve years ago. Shot him down like a

dog. I won't be responsible for anything that
might happen to him while he's in this town. Do
you understand?"

"I'm gonna kill you, Adams," Dell Curry said,
speaking for the first time. "I'm gonna kill you
slow."

"Dell!" the old man snapped. He hadn't looked
at me once, and I didn't think he had any intention
of doing so.

The old man turned and walked away and Dell
Curry reluctantly followed. Dave and Don hurried
away from the bar to catch up to their father and
older brother.

"I never saw that much hatred on one man's
face before," Bat said.

"Dell thought a lot of his older brother," I
explained.

"I wasn't talking about Dell," Bat said, and I
just nodded and finished my beer.

SIX

We had one more beer and then Bat offered to have his girl, Bonnie, get me a friend of hers for the night. I was going to say no, but then I got to thinking about Maggie Harris and I agreed, with a condition.

"Not for the night."

"Whatever you want, Clint. You go on to your room and I'll talk to Bonnie. Shouldn't be too long. You got a preference?"

"Whatever appeals to you," I said, pushing back my chair.

"Well, I won't send you Bonnie, but I'll get you something mighty close."

"Fine."

I started for the door and was aware that more than a few sets of eyes were following me.

"Clint," Bat called.

"Yeah?"

"It's kind of dark out, you know," he reminded me.

"I know it, Bat," I assured him. "Thanks."

I didn't figure on the Currys lying in wait for me

outside in the dark. They weren't saints, but they weren't back shooters, either. Not that I remembered, anyway. The old man had changed a lot since I last saw him, but had he changed that much?

I took a deep breath and walked out through the batwing doors. I hesitated just outside, and when there were no shots, I stepped down from the boardwalk and headed for the hotel.

When I reached the hotel and entered, I let out that deep breath. The old man still ruled with an iron hand, or Dell Curry would have come at me or called me out for sure. First, they'd talk it over, and then they'd make a move, either before the fights, or after. If the old man was serious about wanting his boy to be champ, they would almost surely wait until after all of the fights were over.

I was pretty certain now that I wouldn't have to worry about the Currys—at least, not personally— until then.

Up in my room I removed my hat and gunbelt and lay down on the bed to wait. Women were what I missed most when I was traveling. I rarely paid for a woman, because there were enough willing women around if you looked. I had no doubt that Bat would send me a whore, but since I wasn't paying, I didn't mind.

When the knock came on the door I called out for whoever it was to come in, while I allowed my hand to hover near my gun, which was hanging on the bedpost.

"You're not gonna shoot me, are you?" the girl asked, closing the door behind her.

"Not a chance, pretty lady," I said, dropping my hand.

"Are you Clint Adams?" she asked.

"I am," I said. "Come closer, into the light, so I can see you."

She laughed throatily and said, "I don't think you'll be very disappointed."

She stepped into the light, and she was right. I wasn't very disappointed at all. She was a plump blond, plump in all the right places. I like women with a fair amount of meat on them, and she had her fair share. She wasn't very tall, maybe five-four or so, and she had rounded breasts and fleshy hips.

"You're right," I assured her.

She laughed again and began to remove her clothing. I watched, because watching women undress is a favorite pastime of mine. It builds up the anticipation.

When her breasts were free, I saw that they were heavy, with full, rounded undersides. Her nipples were pink, and her pubic hair was as blonde as the hair on her head. Her hips and thighs were fleshy, but she was only about twenty or so, and she wouldn't have any problems keeping them under control now. Ten years from now, perhaps, she'd be too heavy, but right at that moment, she was just fine.

Naked, she said, "Your turn, now."

I stood up to undress and she turned down the bed and got in. When I was naked also, I slid in next to her. I could feel the heat of her before our bodies even touched.

She reached down and took hold of me and approval was plain on her face.

"I'm not disappointed, either," she said.

"I'm glad."

I reached for her breasts and, as she stroked me, I tweaked her nipples, and then rolled them around in my mouth.

"Mmm, yeah," she said, holding me behind the neck with her free hand.

I slid my hand down over the rise of her belly until my fingers were tangled in those fine, blond hairs. I used one finger to locate her clit, then began to roll it around in a circular motion. Her breathing increased and she began moving her hips against my hand. Her right hand gripped me tightly and began pulling on me rather then stroking me.

"Oh, mister, I'm ready," she whispered.

I dipped one finger into her and found that she was indeed wet and ready.

I threw the sheet off of us and moved to straddle her. She kept me in her hand and guided me to her damp portal. She moved her hand away then and opened her legs wide and I plunged myself into her roughly.

"Ohh," she moaned aloud, and then she wrapped her strong legs around me.

I decided not to hold back and began to bang away at her while she just wrapped her arms around me as well as her legs and held on.

As my tempo increased, her moans became higher in pitch until I thought she might have even been crying. Suddenly she began to writhe wildly beneath me and before her orgasm could end I hurried to catch up with her.

"Oh, God," she said aloud, "it's so hot, and so good."

I was sure she had said the same words before, time and again, and I wished I knew if she were just acting or if she was really enjoying herself. Then again, I supposed that it really didn't matter all that much, either way.

When I rolled off her her breasts were heaving as she tried to catch her breath.

"That was nice," she said, finally.

"Yeah," I said.

"You want me to stay the night, mister?" she asked.

"No," I answered. "I just got into town today and I need my rest. I'm not as young as I used to be."

"Oh, mister, you ain't old," she said, reaching down between my legs again. "If you're tired, you can just lie there. I don't mind doing some of the work."

She slid down until she was crouched between my legs, and when she started to go to work with her teeth, lips and tongue, I had to agree with her.

I wasn't all that old, after all.

SEVEN

Three fighters had been injured since training started for Bat's tournament, and Bat had given me all of their names and where they lived that first night.

I decided to combine a visit to one of them with some exercise for Duke.

Willie Pearson lived on a small ranch just outside of Willow Falls and, according to Bat, was hoping for a shot at Mike McCoole so he could make some money to buy himself a larger spread. Pearson was thirty—a little old to start fighting—and he was married and had two children. He had taken to training inside his barn, and one day when his wife came out to call him for lunch, she found him lying on the floor of the barn, unconscious. Apparently, a bale of hay had fallen from above, injuring his neck and knocking him out. The town doctor had pronounced him unfit to fight in a ring.

Pearson was out of the tournament.

Why would the Harrises or Currys—or anyone else—have feared an inexperienced thirty-year-old rancher? Certainly he was one of the least dangerous opponents.

I rode out to the Pearson ranch and talked to Willie Pearson. He sat through most of the conversation, and it was plain that his neck was bothering him.

I asked Pearson what made him tell Bat Masterson that what had happened to him was no accident.

"There was no reason for that hay bale to be up there," his wife spoke up before her husband had a chance to. "Somebody had to have put it up there, and then dropped it on Willie."

"I never put that bale of hay up there, Mr. Adams," Pearson added.

"Well, he's lucky he wasn't hurt bad," his wife said, "so I'm glad it happened."

"Excuse me," I said, staring at her, "but you're glad that it happened?" I didn't understand that.

"Ella didn't want me to fight, Mr. Adams," Pearson explained. "She was afraid I'd get hurt bad. I was only doing it to try and get us a little more money."

"Well, I'm satisfied with the way things are right now," his wife said. "You can just forget all about prizefighting."

Pearson gave me a pained look, and when I left I wasn't sure what was hurting him more, his neck or his wife's tongue.

EIGHT

The second injured fighter's name was Henry Burton, and he lived back in town. He was a clerk in the general store, and he was one of the young local boys who saw a big opportunity for themselves. Burton, twenty-three, had been closing up the store one night when something hit him on the back of the head, knocking him out of the competition, as well as knocking him out. Again, it was a case of something falling from above—in this case, from a high shelf.

"No way that could have fallen on me by accident, Mr. Adams," Burton assured me. "Me and Mr. Higgins, the owner of the store, are very careful when we put anything up on the high shelves that they are up there securely."

I figured the boy was lucky, because he certainly wasn't built to take on the likes of Billy Harris or Don Curry. He would probably have had trouble staying a round with Ben Neal.

"Did you hear anyone in the store before you were knocked out?" I asked.

"I didn't hear a thing."

"How bad were you hit?"

"I got hit on top of the head. The doc says I'll be all right, but I been having dizzy spells and every once in a while I see double."

He was dejected, but he was a lucky man not to have to face Don Curry, who would probably have hurt him a lot worse.

"What was it that hit you on the head, by the way?" I asked.

"It was a roll of steel wire fencing," he said. He bent his head to show me that he was still wearing a bandage.

"Somebody hurt me, Pearson and Bob Holman on purpose, Mr. Adams. I hope you find out who it was."

"That's what I'm trying to do, Henry. Thanks for your time."

Bob Holman also lived in town, and in injuring him, whoever was behind it could have put an end to the whole tournament. Holman's father was the mayor, and it had taken a lot of fast talking by Bat Masterson to keep him from canceling the whole thing.

I went to the mayor's house to talk to Bob Holman. His injury was not as serious as the other two, but it was to his hand, so naturally he couldn't hope to be ready to box in the tournament.

I asked him how his accident had happened.

"I was out back, Mr. Adams, repairing mother's sulky. I had it propped up firmly, so I know that it couldn't have just slipped and fallen on me. Someone had to have caused it to fall, right on my hand."

He held up his right hand to show me the bandage. "Was it broken?"

"Just badly bruised and sprained," he said. Holman was tall enough to be a fighter, but he needed a good forty pounds or more to beef him up.

"You're probably better off, son," I told him, patting him on the shoulder. That had been what I wanted to tell the other two, as well.

"What do you mean?" he asked. "I could've done well."

"Yes, of course you could have," I said. "Thanks for your time."

*　*　*

None of the three injured "fighters" would have been able to put a dent in either Billy Harris or Don Curry. That much was obvious, so why would the Harrises or Currys have thought it necessary to keep them from fighting? Just to save time? Was their meeting so inevitable that one of them simply decided to speed it up?

If that was indeed the reason, I would have had to lean towards the Currys. Billy Harris looked much too innocent, and he probably only did what his sister told him to do.

Maybe it was time for me and Maggie Harris to have that little talk. The sooner I could eliminate her, the sooner I could concentrate on the Currys.

Although I would much rather have concentrated solely on Maggie Harris, herself.

NINE

I assumed I would find Billy Harris training behind the livery stable and, if that were the case, I'd also find Maggie Harris there.

My assumption was only half right. I found Billy Harris, all right, moving around, dancing, flicking his jab out as if he were boxing his own shadow, but Maggie Harris was nowhere to be seen.

"Hello, Billy," I called out.

He stopped and looked around, and when he saw me he smiled uncertainly.

"Do I know you?" he asked.

"I don't think we were formally introduced, but I did meet your sister."

"You did?" he said, frowning as if he were trying to remember if she had mentioned it. Then his face brightened and he said, "You're that gunfighter fella, aren't you?"

"What?"

"Oh, what did Maggie call you?" he asked himself.

"I'm co-promoting the bouts with Bat Masterson," I pointed out.

"Oh, that too," he said, "but Maggie said that she heard your name before. I know!" he said, looking excited. "The Gunsmith, that's what she called you!"

So she'd finally remembered. I guess I should have expected it. I didn't dwell on it, though, because there was something else bothering me just then.

Billy Harris was twenty-two years old. I knew that because Bat had told me so, but he didn't act like a twenty-two-year-old man. Also, the expression on his face was . . . blank, sort of like a child who has nothing to worry about.

His eyes were vacant, guileless.

"Are you really a gunfighter?" he asked with a child's innocence.

"No, not really, Billy," I said. "I'm more of a gunsmith."

"Then that must be why they call you that," he said, looking proud of himself.

"I guess so," I replied, smiling. I was about to go on when his sister's voice called out from behind me.

"Billy!"

His whole expression changed when he heard her voice. He looked like he'd been caught with his hand in the candy jar at the general store.

Maggie Harris came up next to me and said to her brother, "You're supposed to be working. Can't I leave you alone for five minutes—"

"It wasn't the boy's fault," I cut in. "I interrupted his routine."

She glared at me for a moment, then returned

her eyes to her brother and said, "Go back to work, Billy."

"Yes, Maggie," he mumbled. "It was nice talking to you, sir."

"Same here, Billy. Maybe we can talk again, some other time."

"I'd like—"

"Billy!" his sister snapped, and he backed away and started back in on his routine.

"Mr. Adams—" she began, turning her full attention to me.

"I thought we were beyond that point, Maggie," I said, interrupting her before she could tear into me the same way she did him.

"I don't—"

"And especially since you've remembered where you heard my name before," I added.

She stopped, looked at her brother, and then back at me.

"Billy told you."

"Yes, he did."

"Billy talks too much sometimes," she said. "I have to be around him all the time."

"All the time?" I said. "Does that mean that we can't get together to have our talk?"

"Our talk?"

"You mentioned something about us having a talk, since I'm the co-promoter and all." She didn't answer, so I added, "I'd like to get to know your brother better, as well."

"Maybe we can talk," she said suddenly, as if she'd just made the decision. "What about dinner tonight? We can talk during dinner."

"And after," I added.

She smiled then, the first time I'd seen her smile. Her cheekbones were very high and prominent, and smiling hollowed her cheeks even more. There were small lines at the corner of her eyes that were probably worry lines. They couldn't have been laugh lines. Not with the obvious value she'd put on her smiles, to date.

"Where are you staying?" I asked. "I'll pick you up."

"Why don't I meet you at your hotel, in the lobby," she countered. "Say at seven?"

A stronge willed woman, used to getting her own way.

"Let's make it seven-thirty," I said, trying for a small victory.

Her face hardened, and then softened again as she said, "Very well, Clint. Seven-thirty."

"See you then."

I would have waved at Billy, but he was keeping his eyes studiously to the ground, watching his shadow.

"Keep your left working," she shouted at him, and I walked away leaving brother and sister to their work.

TEN

I went looking for Bat and found him in his room, doing some paperwork.

He looked up from the table he was working at and said, "I'm starting to think maybe you got the easy job and I got the hard one."

He dropped the pencil he was writing with and sat back.

"Entry fees, ticket sales, money for advertising—" He stopped short, and then said, "What's on your mind? Find out something already?"

"I found out something you should have told me," I said.

"Oh? What's that?"

"Billy Harris. He's twenty-two and he's got the mind of a child."

"What are you talking about?"

"Haven't you spoken with him?"

"We haven't said more than two words to each other since they got to town. Maggie does all the talking. What do you mean he's got the mind of a child?"

I explained about the conversation we were having until Maggie showed up.

"If what you say is true, then Maggie's been trying to keep people away from him so nobody would find out."

"I guess so."

" 'Course, if you are right, then maybe he's just simpleminded enough to do exactly like his sister says with no questions asked," Bat proposed.

"You mean like hurting somebody? I don't know if Maggie Harris is that kind of a woman, but I'll find out tonight."

"Tonight?" he asked with interest. "How's that?"

"I've a dinner date with her."

"With Maggie Harris?" he said, looking surprised. "Well, I'll be . . ."

"We're going to talk, Bat," I said.

"You can talk just as well lying down as you can standing up," he pointed out. "I didn't think anybody could get to that iceberg."

"I haven't gotten to her," I pointed out.

"You're gonna try, though."

I stared at him for a few seconds, then grinned and said, "Yeah, I guess I am at that."

ELEVEN

I left my room to go down to the lobby at seven-forty and Maggie Harris was already there, waiting impatiently—which was just what I had in mind.

"I'm not used to being kept waiting, Mr. Adams," she said, jumping on me before I had finished descending the stairs.

"Mr. Adams?" I asked. "Are we back to that, now?" She took a deep breath but before she could explode at me I said, "All right, Maggie. I'm sorry I kept you waiting. I guess my watch is slow. Shall we go to dinner?"

I extended my arm for her to slip hers through, but she turned on her heels and stalked out ahead of me. I looked at the desk clerk, shrugged, and followed, enjoying the rear view.

"Shall we try the café?" I asked, catching up to her.

"Is there anywhere else to eat?" she asked.

We continued on to the café in silence and I wondered just how much talking we would get done that evening. I decided to smoke the peace pipe with her, so I could do what I was really in town to do. Whatever I achieved after that would be gravy.

When we were seated I said, "Before we order dinner I would like to bury the hatchet, Maggie."

"What do you mean?"

"I want to make friends, make amends. If we're going to get anything accomplished this evening, we'll at least have to be on speaking terms. Don't you agree?"

She narrowed her eyes at me suspiciously and said, "Just what it is you hope to accomplish?"

"Not what you're thinking," I assured her. "Look, let your guard down a minute and I'll play it straight with you. You know about the accidents that have occurred involving three of the other fighters.

"Hah," she snorted. "Fighters! More like farmers, and clerks."

"Okay, so they weren't fighters," I agreed. "Then why would someone want to injure them and force them out of the tournament?"

"Injure them?" she said, frowning. "You just said they were accidents."

"They're supposed to be, but that's not the story I get from the injured parties."

"What are you, a detective or something?"

I gave her a reproachful look and said, "You recognized my name, Maggie, so you know I'm not a detective. I'm just an old lawman and a friend of Bat Masterson's. Bat asked me to stick around and look into things, so he could continue to concentrate on the business end of things."

"I see. Do you think I can help you somehow?"

"Well, you're an intelligent woman. I thought you might be able to shed some light on things, since you've been here longer than I have."

She looked at me closely, trying to figure out whether or not I was serious.

"Shall we order dinner and then talk?" I asked. She agreed.

For the next twenty minutes or so, we didn't dig at each other once. We had a serious conversation about the situation in town, and I discovered that she was indeed not only intelligent, but shrewd as well.

Her choice for the guilty parties was, of course, the Currys.

"They're mean enough. At least, the old man and his oldest son are. The younger two just seem to follow the older two around."

"Would you agree that the three injured men would have had no chance again Don Curry—or against your brother, for that matter?"

"Of course I'd agree. Those three—" then she stopped short and looked at me hard, and I knew the conversation was going to regress at least twenty minutes. "You suspect me, too, don't you? Me and Billy?"

"I suspect everyone, Maggie. Don't get your back up."

"Why you—"

"Tell me about Billy, Maggie," I said, interrupting her. The question threw her off balance, catching her with her mouth open.

"Billy," she said. "What about Billy?"

"Physically he's twenty-two," I said, "but how old is he mentally?"

She stiffened and said, "I don't know what you're talking about."

"Maggie, come on. I spoke with the boy this

afternoon. You haven't let anyone get near him since you arrived in town. Why don't you want anyone to talk to him? Why'd you interrupt us this afternoon?" I leaned forward and said, "His mind is not twenty-two years old, is it, Maggie?"

"I don't see what that has to do with anything. You can't suspect Billy just because his mind is—is not—"

"What's the word they used back East, Maggie? Simple?"

She stared at me, then lowered her head and said, "That and some fancy medical names. His mind just hasn't grown up like the rest of him," she said. "It's like he's had to pay for being as big and strong as he is."

"That's not anything to be ashamed of, Maggie. He seemed like a decent boy when I spoke to him."

"Then how could you suspect him?" she asked.

"I didn't say I suspected him," I said. I was about to go on when the look on her face made me stop.

"I see," she said, staring at me. Then "I see," again. "You don't suspect Billy. You suspect me. You think I told Billy to hurt those men, and he did because he's simpleminded."

"Maggie, go easy. I told you I suspect everyone. I have to. And you have to admit, Billy does whatever you tell him to do."

"I take care of him," she said. "I don't tell him to hurt people."

"Outside the ring, you mean," I added.

"Fighting is all Billy can do, Clint," she said.

"He's good at it, but he has to be pushed, because he *doesn't* like to hurt people."

"You still think he can be champ, with that kind of thinking?"

"You said it before," she answered. "He does what I tell him to do. So your big question is, did I tell him to hurt those men."

"I guess it is," I agreed.

We sat there in silence for a short time while she tried to decide whether to answer my "big question" or not.

Finally, she made her choice.

"All right. I did not tell Billy to hurt those men. I didn't have to, Clint. He wouldn't have had any problem with any of them so it wouldn't have done us any good."

"I guess the same can be said for the Currys," I pointed out.

"That may be, but I'm answering for me, not them. Billy didn't touch those men."

I hesitated a moment, then realized that I had to say something, so I said, "All right."

"Do you believe me?"

I was hoping she wouldn't ask me that.

"I'd like to, Maggie," I said. "Believe me, I'd like to."

TWELVE

"So?" Bat asked me the next morning at breakfast.

"So what?"

"How did it go?"

"Oh, you mean with Maggie?"

"Of course I mean with Maggie," he said.

"It went all right."

"Only all right?" he asked, looking disappointed.

"We snapped at each other for a while, then we had a nice long talk. I think we got along."

"Got along, or got along?" he asked.

"I walked her to the rooming house where she's staying, Bat, and then I came home. That's it."

He gave me a look that said he didn't believe me—or didn't want to believe me—but that was just what happened. As much as Bat was expecting me to make some kind of effort to bed Maggie Harris the night before, I think Maggie also expected it. That may have been the major reason why I didn't try. Once again, I had thrown her off balance by simply walking her to her door, and then saying good night.

Let her think about it for a while, I decided. If it happened, it would probably be worth the wait for both of us.

"Come on," Bat said.

"Think what you like," I said, "but nothing happened."

"Okay," Bat said, but the look on his face said he still didn't buy it. "What did you find out?"

I explained that I had played it straight with Maggie and asked her for her own suspicions, and then went on to tell him how we got on the subject of Billy.

"It became apparent at a young age that Billy's mind wasn't growing at the same rate he was," I explained. "When their parents died, Billy was only eight, so Maggie took over raising him, and she's been taking care of him, sheltering him ever since."

"Making a fighter out of him."

"She says that's all he can do, and he doesn't like to do it. He doesn't like hurting people."

"And she expects to make him a champ?"

"Well, we were right about one thing. He does what she tells him to do virtually without question."

"Which brings us right back to where we started from," he said.

"She pointed out that there was no reason for her to tell Billy to hurt those men. He could have taken care of any one of them in the ring."

"The same goes for Don Curry."

I nodded, and this time I said, "Which brings us right back to where we started from."

"Not a very good place to be," Bat said.

"I guess I'll have to talk to the Currys," I said.

Bat made a face and said, "Sure, leave your gun in your room, too, while you're at it. Make it real easy for them."

"Oh, I don't think I'll have any trouble just yet."

"Your faith in human nature astounds me," he said. "What makes you think that?"

"I'll just tell old Dan that if he doesn't cooperate with me, the whole thing might be called off. If he's serious about wanting his youngest to be champ, he'll cooperate."

I got up to leave and Bat said, "Now?"

"It's as good a time as any."

"Good luck, friend," he said. "You're going to need it."

THIRTEEN

I went looking for the Currys.

Bat had already told me that they'd taken over an abandoned ranchhouse outside of town, so I went to the stable and saddled Duke up.

Going out there alone may not have been a great idea, but I really thought that the only one I might have to worry about was the hothead, Dell Curry. As long as the old man was there, though, he'd keep Dell in line. The Currys wouldn't have traveled all this way unless they were serious about Don being a boxer and meeting Mike McCoole.

I was counting on Dan Curry not wanting to spoil that opportunity.

As I approached the ranch, I could see a ring roped off outside of the main house with two men inside of it. As I got closer I realized that Don and Dave were in the ring, while Old Dan and Dell were outside, watching. There wasn't much difference between the two boys in the ring, but Don was a little taller and broader.

They were all so intent on what was going on

inside the ring that they didn't notice me until I had stopped behind Dan and Dell.

It was Don who saw me first, and the others turned to see what he was looking at.

"Adams!" Dan snapped.

Dell actually went for his gun and got his hand on it, but an instant before I would have gone for mine, Dan clamped a frail hand on his oldest boy's gun arm.

"He'll kill you, boy," he said.

Angrily, Dell pulled his arm away and said, "I can take him, Pa!" He did not make another attempt to pull his gun, however. He just stood there and glared at me.

The other two boys came over to the rope and Dan said to all three of them, "Just settle down." He turned to me and said, "What the hell do you want, Adams?"

"I want to ask you some questions," I said.

"I don't answer your questions," he said. "In fact, I don't even talk to you, mister. Now turn that horse of yours around before I let my boys loose."

"You'll answer my questions, Dan, or there'll be no boxing matches held."

"Pa—" Don, the youngest, began, but Dan held up his hand and the boy fell silent.

"What the hell you talkin' about?"

"So-called accidents have taken out three of the local fighters, Dan. One of them was the mayor's son. I was brought in to find out what's been happening here. If I don't, the mayor just might call the whole thing off."

"He can't," Dan said. "We done paid our money already."

"Well, the mayor will just make Masterson give you your money back," I said.

He stared at me coldly while his mind raced, trying to decide whether I was telling the truth or not.

"All right," he said finally. "Ask your questions, but stay on your horse and clear out when you've got your answers."

I played it as straight with Curry as I had with Maggie Harris. I told him there was some question as to whether or not the "accidents" were really that. I tried to watch all of their faces while I spoke, but Dan's and Dell's were too clouded by hatred to betray anything else. The other two just looked puzzled.

"Adams, you see my boy," Dan Curry said, pointing to Don. "Do you think he'd be afraid of a couple of farm boys or store clerks?" It was the same thing Maggie'd said.

"No, I can't say that he would, Dan. But wouldn't you like to make things just a little bit easier for him?"

"I don't have to," he said. "My boy likes to fight, Adams. He'd be mad as hell if I deprived him of one more fight."

I looked at Don Curry, who was nodding his head to indicate his agreement. He began to pound his right fist into his left hand for good measure.

"Now does that answer all of your questions?" Dan Curry demanded.

"Not all of them," I said, "but enough for now."

"Enough forever," Dell Curry broke in. "Don't come back here again, Adams. Next time I'll kill you!"

"No you won't, Dell," I said, turning Duke around. "You can't even wipe your ass unless your daddy tells you to. So long, boys."

I swore I could feel Dell's eyes burning into my back all the way back to town.

FOURTEEN

When I got back to town I put Duke up at the livery again and went to the saloon. Bat wasn't there, and there was no poker game in sight, so I got a beer from the bartender—apparently Ben was off that night—and took the mug to a corner table.

I was thinking that the situations in the Curry and Harris families were remarkably alike. Billy would do whatever Maggie told him to do, and the same went for Dell, who would obey Dan without question.

It was time to put the Currys and Harrises aside, I decided, and check on some of the other competitors. It might make more sense to believe that some of them wanted to pare down the field a bit, giving them a better chance to succeed. There were other out-of-towners as well as several other local boys who were going to give it a try. They would all have to be checked out before I could point a finger at anybody.

I pushed away from the table to get up and leave when I saw that Ben Neal had taken up his place behind the bar after all. This might be a good time to get some use out of him.

I took my empty mug over to the bar and asked him to fill it up again.

"Ben, maybe you can help me out a little," I said when he put the mug of beer in front of me.

"Sure," he said, eagerly.

"What can you tell me about some of the local boys who are involved in these fights? Any of them got a chance?"

"Naw, not against the Curry and Harris boys."

"Would any of the locals try to . . . even up the odds a little?" I asked.

"What do you mean?"

"I mean would they hurt someone, force him out of the competition, to give themselves a better chance?"

He rubbed his jaw. "Let me think. Nobody rightly comes to mind who'd be rotten enough to do it. Let me think," he said again. I nursed my beer while Ben Neal walked back and forth behind the bar, serving customers and frowning fiercely, deep in thought.

Finally he came over to me. "I can only come up with one name."

"That's a start."

"Jedediah Hunt," he said. "Jed's the blacksmith in town, a giant of a man who thinks maybe becoming champ could be his ticket away from horseshoes and the forge."

"How bad does he want it?"

"Pretty bad. He says he'll break the back of any man who gets in the ring with him."

"What does he think we're putting on, wrestling matches?" I asked.

"Jed's got fists the size of hams," Ben said. "He could break your back by hitting you in front. If you're gonna talk to him, I'd be mighty careful what I say and how I say it."

"I'll keep that in mind," I said. I pushed the empty mug towards him and said, "Keep thinking on it, will you, Ben?"

"I surely will, Clint. If I come up with something else, I'll find you."

"Good enough. Thanks."

As if I didn't have enough trouble, I went out looking for more.

FIFTEEN

Jed Hunt stood at least six-seven, which would make him tower over either Billy Harris or Don Curry, but size didn't really mean anything. If he didn't know anything about boxing, either man would be able to pick him apart. He was busily at work when I entered the livery, and I waited for a lull in his activity before stepping up and asking him a silly question.

"Are you Jed Hunt?"

He turned slowly and looked at me, seeming to scowl from beneath bushy black eyebrows. He was bushy almost everywhere, with curly black hair covering his arms and his chest.

"Who wants to know?" he asked.

"My name is Clint Adams. I don't know whether or not you've heard, but I'm co-promoting the boxing matches next week. I understand you're an entrant."

"I'm a what?"

"Uh, you're one of the fighters?"

"That's right," he said. "I'm the man that's gonna win. Ain't nobody stronger than me." He said it proudly and pounded his chest with one massive fist.

"Well, if you'll excuse me for saying so," I said cautiously, "it takes more than strength and size to win a fight."

"I know that," he said. "I got a brain, too."

"That helps," I admitted, "but have you got any boxing skills?"

"I can hit," he said, "but I got a plan."

"Can I ask what that plan is?" It occurred to me that this man might be dim enough to confess that his plan was to eliminate all the other entrants before the competition began. His answer made me wonder whether I'd overestimated him.

"I let them do the hittin'," he said, "until they get tired. Then it's my turn."

I stared at him to make sure he was serious, and he was.

"Let them hit you?"

"I can take whatever they can dish out," he said confidently.

If he expected to get to the championship that way, even if he made it, he wouldn't have much of a face left, or a head . . . or a brain.

"That's a plan, all right," I said. "What about knocking some of them out of the competition before the fights even begin?"

He stared at me, then frowned. "But that wouldn't be fair."

"No, it wouldn't," I agreed. "I suppose that idea never occurred to you?"

"You asking me if I'd cheat?" he demanded, looking indignant. He stepped away from his work and towards me, and I backed up a cautious step.

"I don't never cheat, mister," he said. "Not at nothing. I ain't never cheated."

"Of course not, Jedediah. I didn't mean to imply that you had."

"It sounded like you meant it," he said. "Maybe I should fix it so you ain't around for the fights."

"That wouldn't be smart," I said.

"Why not?" he asked, taking a step towards me.

"Because," I said, taking a step back, "if I am not there, then there will be no boxing matches."

He frowned, and stood his ground, neither stepping forward or back.

"Why are you so important?"

I explained what my job was, and about the accidents. He frowned again, and then said, "I ain't hurt anybody, mister, and I don't plan to—until I step into the ring, that is. Then I'll wade my way through anybody what stands between me and Mike McCoole. Once I'm finished with him, I'll be champ. I'll be famous, and I won't have to work here no more. I'll be able to travel all over the country, and maybe even the world."

"But you wouldn't cheat to get what your after."

He shook his head. "That wouldn't be fair."

I believed him. He wasn't brilliant, but he believed in playing fair.

SIXTEEN

I spent the rest of the day talking to the other entrants, both local and out of town. I tried to get a feel for them, of what they were like. Most of them seemed to be in the tournament because it was there and why not give it a shot? A few thought they might have had a decent chance if it wasn't for Harris and Curry. Most of them seemed to be afraid of the Curry clan, but simply cautious about Billy Harris. Either way, it made no sense to suspect any of them of causing the accidents.

I hoped I wasn't going to have to wait for a fourth accident before I knew for sure who was behind them.

Just before sundown I wandered over to the livery stable again to have a chat.

"Hello, Billy."

He stopped fighting his shadow and looked over at me.

"I-I can't talk to you," he said, staring at the ground.

"I understand, Billy," I told him. "It's all right.

I want to talk to your sister. Can you just tell me where she is?"

He thought it over a moment, then apparently figured there was no harm.

"She's at the boardinghouse."

"Okay, thanks."

He went back to work, and I walked over to the boardinghouse. I was about to knock on the door when I heard some kind of commotion around the side. Following the sound I found Maggie Harris and Dell Curry. Dell, ever the ladies' man, was trying his luck with Maggie, but she wasn't having any, and Dell wasn't about to take no for an answer.

"Come on, Maggie," he was saying as she fought to escape the circle of his arms.

"Let me go, Curry, or—"

"Or what?" he asked, laughing. "You'll sic your little brother on me? I'd eat that kid up alive and spit him out. Now come on, relax a little."

"Let her go, Dell."

"What?" he said, turning his head to see who was speaking. When he spotted me he let her loose, but not because I had told him to. Seeing me, he had momentarily lost all interest in her. His hatred for me overpowered his lust for her.

"Adams!" he snapped, and I could see that he wanted nothing less than to go for his gun. I figured he wouldn't. I figured he knew his Pa would lash into him if he did. Which meant I could have gone for mine and killed him right there.

"Move on, Dell. The lady and I have an appointment," I said evenly.

"I got here first, Adams. She's mine."

"I think we ought to let the lady choose, don't you?"

"No, I don't. I ain't gonna draw on you, Adams. My Pa don't want you dead yet." He took a step towards me and continued, "And I don't think you'll shoot me, knowing that I ain't going for my gun, so I think I'll jes walk on up to you and stomp the shit outta you!"

"Dell—" I said warningly, but he was right. I wasn't going to shoot him down. It would be like shooting an unarmed man.

I was going to have to fight him.

I remembered years ago, being in a similar situation with his brother, Dan Jr. Back then, Dan had stomped the shit out of me, and had almost killed me. I supposed that Dell was of the opinion that, when I got back to my feet, I went looking for Dan Jr. specifically to kill him, in return for that beating.

He remembered, too.

"My brother stomped you good, Adams," he said, grinning tightly, "and I'm gonna do the same."

"Dell, you aren't the man your brother was, and you'll never be. I know it . . . and your Pa knows it."

He knew it, all right, and he didn't like being reminded of it.

He came at me in a mad rush, like a wounded bull, half blinded by pain and rage. I sidestepped him and thrust out one foot so that he tripped over it and went sprawling in the dirt.

"You're clumsy, Dell," I said. "If your little brother is as clumsy as you, he's got no business being in the ring."

I wanted to keep him angry, because he was bigger and stronger than me, and given half a chance, he *would* stomp me just like his older brother had years before.

He scrambled to his feet and fixed me with a malevolent glare. His face was covered with dirt, but he didn't bother to brush it away. He began to advance on me, slowly now, but the rage was still in his eyes. He threw a big roundhouse right that I ducked underneath, and I hit him with a short left in the ribs. I knew he had a rock-hard belly just by looking at him, so I didn't bother with it. If I could bruise his ribs, though, that would slow him down some.

He grunted from the blow, then swung a left at me. We were so close that his left only hit me on my right arm, but it made the arm go numb. I could still move it, but I couldn't feel it. If he hit me there again, the arm would be as good as dead. I didn't enjoy that prospect, because that was my gun arm.

I backed away from him to regain my balance. He kept advancing, but now the sweat forming on his brow was mixing with the dirt on his face, and together they were falling into his eyes. He began to blink rapidly as the mixture affected his eyesight, and I immediately took advantage of the situation. I moved in and swung a vicious, hard left right at his face, catching him on the side of the jaw. He took the punch well, staggering back a few feet, without falling. I followed up without giving him a chance to get his bearings. I used the left again, not wanting to damage my right further. I hit him in the same spot and this time he did go down, but only to one knee. I hit him on the other side of the face, using my knee, and knocked him onto his back, where he lay, stunned, but not out.

Maggie came over and looked down at him, then looked up at me. "Aren't you going to finish him?"

I shook my head. "It is finished."

She stared at me a moment and then said, "No killer instinct," in disgust.

"You're welcome, Maggie."

SEVENTEEN

I took Maggie by the arm and steered her off before Dell Curry could regain his senses—or what little sense he had.

"Where are we going?" she asked, trotting to keep up with me.

"Somewhere we can talk," I said.

"Let's go to the livery stable. I want to check on Billy."

"Billy's fine. Let's go to the café and have a cup of coffee," I said.

She started to protest, then lapsed into a suspicious silence. She had something up her sleeve, or she would have been arguing with me. She just wasn't the type of woman who would come along quietly.

When we got to the café she allowed me to order two cups of coffee.

"You're welcome," I said to her again.

"Oh, that!" she said. "All right, thank you, but I could have handled him myself."

Flexing the fingers of my left hand I said, "I wish I had known."

66

"You handled him pretty easily," she said.

"I was lucky."

"No, you were fast and you took advantage of every mistake he made. You were very . . . competent."

"I could also have been very dead," I added. "Dell Curry is a big, strong man who probably would have stomped the life out of me if he'd gotten close enough."

"But you didn't let him."

"Like I said, I was lucky."

"Don't be modest," she said.

I gave her an exasperated look and said forcefully, "I am not being modest, Maggie!"

"Okay, have it your way," she replied, "but I have a proposition for you."

"You do?" I said, wondering if I should ask for some ice to soak my hand in.

"Yes, I do." She waited a moment, to give it the proper amount of dramatic impact, and then said, "I want you to spar with Billy."

I stared at her a moment, then said, "Forget it."

"Now, Clint—"

"Forget it, Maggie."

"But I need you," she said. "I have to get Billy ready, and no one's been able to stand up for more than one round with him."

"I'm not a boxer, Maggie."

"That doesn't matter."

"To you, maybe. I am not going to get into the ring with a boy almost twenty years younger than me and get my head handed to me. Besides, since I'm co-promoter of the contests, it wouldn't be right for me to spar with one of the contestants."

She opened her mouth to argue, then probably realized that I was correct on that point.

"Damn," she said, plopping her chin down into her left hand.

"Then again . . ." I said, letting it trail off.

"What?" she asked, quickly.

"Well, I might be able to help you with a sparring partner—"

"Who?"

"I said *might*, now. Don't get your hopes up. The man I'm thinking about has some idea about fighting himself."

"Who is it?"

I explained about Jed Hunt, and his "battle plan."

"He'll get chopped to pieces fighting that way," she said.

"That's what I figured, but he's big enough to stand up to your brother long enough to spar with. The problem would be convincing him to spar and not to fight."

"He doesn't have to withdraw from the tournament," she said. "The sparring sessions could just as well do him some good, too. I'll talk to him," she said, rising.

"Whoa, slow down, Maggie," I said, putting my hand on her arm. "Don't rush off so fast. You owe me, now."

She hesitated, then sat down.

"For Dell Curry? I told you—"

"For Dell and for Jed Hunt. Come on, now, be fair."

She compressed her lips in annoyance and said,

"All right, but talk fast. I've got to talk to this man, Hunt, and then get back to Billy."

"Your brother was working hard when I saw him," I said, and then quickly added, "and he wouldn't tell me anything but where you were. He wouldn't talk to me at all."

"Good," she said.

I didn't think it was so good, but I let her comment go by.

"I need your help," I told her.

"With what?"

"With finding out who caused all of those accidents."

She smirked and said, "I thought you suspected me."

"I suspect everyone," I said, "but I probably suspect you the least." That wasn't strictly true, but it didn't harm anything to tell her that. "I want to solve this thing before somebody else gets hurt. Who knows, Billy could be next."

That was a sobering thought for her, and she frowned as I made the remark.

"What do you want me to do?"

"Just keep your ears open, I guess. You can get closer to the other fighters and managers than I can."

"What about the Currys? Tell the truth, shouldn't they be your number one suspects?"

"Dell and his old man, maybe. I think the other two are clear."

I explained about the meeting I'd had with them out at the ranch where they were training.

"How did Don Curry look?" she asked.

"He looked real good, Maggie," I said. "In fact, I don't think there would be all that much difference between the three Curry brothers."

"You took Dell," she said. "You took him easy."

"Dell's a hothead. I was able to get him mad enough to make a couple of mistakes. Old Dan is not going to let Don get into the ring without drumming that into his head. Don't get mad enough to make mistakes. Isn't that what you tell Billy?"

"Hah," she laughed. "I wish Billy would get mad."

I knew what she meant. Billy was a gentle boy in the body of a man. He wasn't and wouldn't be mad at any of the men he was fighting.

"No killer instinct," I said.

She looked at me sharply, and then looked away. As far as she was concerned, that was his only flaw.

"Will you help me?"

"Only because of what you said about Billy possibly being the next victim. If somebody is looking to make this thing easier for themselves, getting rid of Billy would be one way. I'll keep my eyes and ears open," she agreed.

"Okay. Thanks. How about letting me buy you dinner? I'll pick you up at the roominghouse at eight. How's that?"

I guess she couldn't think of a reason not to, so she shrugged and said, "If you want."

I wasn't bowled over by her enthusiasm.

EIGHTEEN

I went looking for Bat to tell him that we might have some trouble from the Currys, after my run-in with Dell. I found him at a table in the saloon, staring forlornly at a deck of cards.

"Still can't find anyone to play with you, eh?" I asked, sitting down opposite him.

"This town has no adventure in its soul," he said.

"Either that, or they're too damn smart."

He frowned at me and asked, "What have you been up to?"

I told him about the fight with Dell Curry, and about the agreement with Maggie Harris.

"Well, you seem to know the Currys better than I do," he said when I was finished. "What will they do next?"

"I think old Dan is serious about Don's boxing future, so I don't believe they'll want to jeopardize that by trying to kill me. He'll probably complain to you. Who's the sheriff in this town?" I asked him.

"His name is Ned Tyler, and he's already spoken to me about you."

"He has?"

"Yep. He said he didn't appreciate my bringing in a gunman to play enforcer."

"Maybe I'd better go and have a talk with him." I didn't like being thought of as a gunman, and I liked being called one even less.

"You'll scare the boots off of him," Bat said. "I think that's what he's worried about most, that you'll do something that might require him to take some sort of action. I assured him that you wouldn't."

"Except that Dan Curry might go to him about this," I said.

Bat shrugged.

"Wait and see," he suggested.

I thought it over, then decided to do just that. Bat finished his beer and I signaled Ben to bring over two more. I told Bat to deal the cards and we'd see if anyone would get interested enough to sit in with us. Lucky for him, two out-of-town cowboys rode in and asked us if they could join us. Once the game took up a head of steam, I bowed out, saying that if they were still playing later I might join in again. I left Bat sitting with a wide smile on his face, in his glory.

I went back to the hotel, bathed and changed clothes, and then walked over to meet Maggie at the boardinghouse. I was admitted by the woman who ran the place, who told me to wait in the sitting room and Miss Harris would be right down.

"Such a nice young woman," the elderly woman remarked.

"Yes, ma'am."

"Some man would be very lucky to grab her for a wife," the woman went on.

"Yes, ma'am," I said.

I was just considering waiting outside when Maggie came down and said, "Thank you, Mrs. Halliday."

"You're very welcome, my dear," she said. "Nice to have met you," she said to me.

"Same here, ma'am," I said.

She smiled at both of us and left the room.

Maggie was dressed much the same way she had been, in a shirt and pants.

"Don't you ever wear a dress?" I asked her.

She glared at me and said, "Only on special occasions. Do you want to fight, or have dinner?"

"Let's have dinner," I said.

Over dinner Maggie really talked about herself and Billy, and how things had been since their parents died. She'd had little time for herself while caring for him, little time for buying the right clothes, or for getting married.

"I apologize for my remark about your not wearing a dress," I said as I walked her back to the boarding house.

"That's all right," she said. "I really don't think about it much, anymore—about clothes, I mean, and dressing like a lady should."

"I guess if Billy wins the championship, you'll have more time and money for things like that."

"I suppose. I want to make enough money so that Billy won't have to fight anymore. I'm only hard on him because I want him to win. It will help us both so much."

"I understand."

As we were approaching the boardinghouse I put a hand on her arm to stop her, and she turned towards me. Her face was really relaxed for the first time since I met her, and it was a soft, lovely face, with violet eyes and a full mouth.

"Come back to my hotel with me," I said, putting my hands on her shoulders.

"Why?" she asked. "Because you feel sorry for me?"

"No," I answered, "because I want you."

I kissed her then, and she didn't resist, but neither did she react. I held the kiss for a while longer, and then her lips softened and she leaned into me.

"All right," she said when I broke the kiss, and we turned and walked the other way.

NINETEEN

In bed she was all woman. Soft, responsive, even demanding. Her breasts were large and firm, a wonderful cushion as I lay on top of her, thrusting myself into her. She opened her legs wide to me, gasping each time I penetrated deeper and deeper. It had been a long time for her, I could tell, and I tried to make it as enjoyable for her as I could.

"I've never known a man who wanted to give a woman so much pleasure," she said to me at one point.

"Have you know that many men?" I asked, teasing.

She probably could have taken offense at the remark, but she didn't.

"No, not really," she said. She rolled over onto me and said, "I want to be on top, this time."

I held her buttocks with my hands as she sat atop me. I entered her easily, and she threw her head back, showing me the lovely line of her neck as she rode me. I took her nipples into my mouth one at a time, and then found that her breasts were large enough for me to take both nipples and suck them at the same time. She began to moan aloud when I did that, and she increased the tempo of her hips to such a degree that I could no longer hold back.

I emptied myself into her and she squeezed her eyes shut as she felt the heat of my seed flowing into her.

"Oh, God," she said when I was totally empty, and she lay down on me with her face in my neck. "I needed that," she whispered, "I really needed that. Thank you."

"Thank you," I said.

"Can I go to sleep here?" she asked.

"If you have no regard for your reputation," I said, "you can sleep here all night."

"Shit," she said, letting me know how worried she was about her reputation, and then she went to sleep.

TWENTY

I woke first in the morning and successfully got out of bed without waking Maggie. She had awakened me once during the night to make love again, and then we had slept until morning. I decided to let her wake up on her own, got dressed and went in search of breakfast.

As I was crossing the street to the café, I heard someone call me.

"Mr. Adams?"

I turned and saw Billy Harris bearing down on me, a frantic look on his face.

"Billy, what's wrong?" I asked.

When he reached me he paused, as if to catch his breath, and then he said, "It's Maggie. I can't find her. She didn't come back to the room-inghouse last night after you took her to dinner."

I was stuck. I knew I could quell any fears he might have had about his sister's welfare, but would she want me to tell him exactly where she spent the night? If he were a normal twenty-two-year-old man, with a normal twenty-two-year-old mind, it wouldn't have been a problem.

"Uh, Billy, your sister is just fine. Don't worry," I said, hoping that would be enough.

It wasn't.

"But where is she?" he asked.

"She's all right, Billy—" I started to reassure him, but he grabbed my arm in an iron grip and I stopped.

"Mr. Adams, please," he said. "I'm very worried about my sister. If you know where she is, please tell me."

"Billy!" Maggie's voice called from across the street.

Billy turned his head and we both spotted her at the same time. Apparently, she had woken up just after I left the room and had just come out of the hotel.

"Maggie," he said. I pulled on my arm, trying to free it from his grip, but I couldn't. He wasn't even paying attention to me and his grip was still too strong for me to break.

Maggie ran across the street and when she reached us she grabbed his arm and said, "Billy, let go!"

He was looking at her with such a relieved look on his face that it was almost comical.

"Maggie, you're all right," he said.

"I'm fine," she said, yanking on his arm with both hands now. "Billy, let Clint go!" she snapped.

He looked at his hand on my arm—which was starting to go numb now—and then suddenly let go, as if he hadn't realized how tightly he had been holding it—which, of course, he had not.

"Clint, what happened?" she asked.

"Nothing," I said, massaging my arm. "He was worried about you, wanted to know where you were."

"Oh, no," she whispered.

"I told him you were fine," I said.

"I wanted him to tell me where you were," Billy said. The expression on his face when he looked at his sister was one of pure adoration.

"Of course, I couldn't really tell him. . . ." I said, allowing it to trail off.

"No, that's all right, Clint," she said, touching my arm, looking flustered and confused. "I'll take care of it."

She took her brother's arm and said, "Come on, Billy, we have a lot of work to do."

"But where were you?"

"We'll talk about it," she assured him. "Come with me." She turned to me and said, "We'll talk later."

"Okay."

I watched them walk away, deep in conversation. I had never seen Maggie that confused, and I had never run up against a grip as strong as the one Billy had on my arm. I felt for sure that I had a bruise for every one of his fingers. He certainly looked powerful, but I had no idea he was that strong.

The brother-sister relationship between the two of them was certainly an odd one, and I wondered if I'd ever really understand it.

I went into the café, still thinking about Maggie and Billy Harris, and ordered some eggs and coffee. I didn't realize until after I had sat down and ordered that there was someone else in the room that I knew—in a way, that is.

Sitting on the other side of the room was the youngest of the Curry brothers, Don.

He didn't seem to notice that I was there. Either that or he just didn't recognize me, which might have been understandable. He had seen me as a child, and this week he had seen me twice. Once in the saloon, from across the room, and once at the ranch.

I stood up and walked over to his table.

"Do you mind if I join you?" I asked.

He was already eating his breakfast and he looked up from his plate at me. I couldn't tell whether he recognized me or not, but he said, "Sure, help yourself."

I sat down opposite him and he continued to eat.

"I don't know if you know who I am, Don," I said to him.

He paused with his fork halfway to his mouth and said, "Oh, I know who you are, Adams. You're the man who killed my big brother, Dan."

And he continued eating.

TWENTY-ONE

"You were just a kid when that happened," I said.

"But I remember," he assured me. He leaned his elbow on the table and looked at me while he chewed his food. "I remember being very grateful to you for killing him. Maybe now would be a good time to say thanks, huh?"

He went on eating, as if we were just talking about the price of beef, or something.

"Don, I don't think I understand," I said. "Dan was your brother."

"He was my big brother," he said. "He was Pa's favorite, and he never let us forget it. That is, me and Dave. Dell and him were always real close, just like Dave and I are close, but the four of us were never really that close. Did you know that we have different mothers?"

"No, I didn't know."

"Yeah, me and Dave, we're full brothers, and Dan and Dell were full brothers. It gets confusing when you talk about it, but Dave and me are only half-brothers with Dan and Dell. You understand all of that?"

"I think so. Are you telling me that you don't care that I killed Dan?"

He shrugged with his face and said, "Not much."

"And how close are you and your father?"

He shrugged again, this time using his shoulders as well

"He wants me to be champ, but that don't make us close. He just wants people to respect the name of Curry."

"He should have thought of that a long time ago," I commented.

"Yeah, well, he's thought of it now."

"Would he jeopardize the possibility of your becoming champ?" I asked.

"You mean, would he hurt those other fighters to give me a better chance, but take a chance at being caught?" he asked. When I nodded he said, "No, I don't think so. I've been thinking about it ever since you came out to the ranch. If he got caught, they—you—probably wouldn't let me fight. He wouldn't take that kind of a chance."

I didn't tell him that I would still let him fight if I was sure that he personally had nothing to do with it. I wouldn't make him suffer for what his father and half-brother did.

"What about Dell?"

"You know Dell," he said. "He's just like Dan Jr. was. He won't do anything Pa doesn't tell him to."

"Well, almost," I said. When he frowned at me I explained about what had happened between Dell and me when I found him with Maggie Harris.

He started laughing and choked on the food he

had in his mouth. When he stopped choking he was still laughing, saying, "I wish I could have seen that. Oh, boy! Pa's gonna have a hard time keeping a tight rein on Dell now."

"I don't want to have to kill him," I said.

"From your standpoint that would be a damned sight better than letting him kill you," he remarked.

"I'd like to avoid any killing, either way," I said.

He ate the last of his breakfast and then sat there shaking his head, a small smile on his face.

"Yeah, old Dell has had his eye on Maggie Harris since we got here." He started chuckling and said, "I sure wish I could have seen that."

The waitress set my breakfast down at the table.

"I'm only here for one reason, Mr. Adams," he said, paying the waitress what he owed her. "To win this tournament and to fight Mike McCoole for the championship of the world."

"Do you think you can beat Billy Harris?" I asked.

"Have you ever spoken to him?" he asked, standing up.

"Not at any great length," I hedged.

"Well, take it from me. I've got great respect for his physical ability, but I've got something he doesn't."

"What's that?"

He winked at me and tapped his temple, then walked out.

I went back to my table with the realization that Don Curry knew about Billy Harris's problem. I only hoped that he would keep it to himself.

TWENTY-TWO

The remainder of that day was relatively uneventful—until after dark.

I spent most of my time just watching some of the fighters work out, including Billy Harris. I stayed away from the Currys, as I would continue to do, at least until I found out how they were going to respond to the fight Dell and I had. What I had told Don was true. I didn't want to kill Dell. I had already killed one Curry too many.

I wasn't sure whether I was avoiding Maggie or she was avoiding me, but we managed to keep a respectable distance between us for most of the day. I wondered what she had told Billy about where she had spent the night.

When darkness fell, it found me and Bat in the saloon, and Bat was once again brooding about not being able to get up a poker game.

"What happened to your friends from yesterday?" I asked him.

"They rode out today."

"Did you leave them any money?"

"Some," he said, grinning. Then he sobered

and said, "I wouldn't have, though, if I had known they were going to leave town today."

"Have you seen old Dan Curry today?"

"No. Kind of surprised me, too. I thought after that fight yesterday he'd come in here screaming at me."

At that point the batwing doors opened and two men stepped into the saloon. One of them looked like he wanted to do some screaming. The other one just looked like he wanted to kill somebody.

Preferably me.

"Don't look now," I said, "but you may have been right, yet."

"Huh?" he said, turning in his seat and looking over his shoulder. He spotted Dan Curry just about the time Curry spotted him. Dell had spotted me the minute he walked in, and hadn't taken his eyes from me since. They both started towards our table, and I backed my chair up some.

"Hello, Dan," Bat said.

"Masterson, I told you to keep this man away from my boys and me," Dan bellowed.

"The man has a right to go wherever he feels his job takes him, Dan."

"Yeah? Well, he near beat my boy to death yesterday," Dan went on, and Dell gave his father an angry look for mentioning it in front of a saloon full of people. He had livid bruises on both sides of his face, so that no one would have any trouble trying to guess which boy Dan was talking about.

"I've got a mind to go right to the sheriff," Dan continued.

"You do what you think you've got to do, Dan,

but that would mean that the sheriff would have to hear the same story I did. You want Maggie Harris to tell her side of the story, as well?"

Dan compressed his lips and surpressed rage turned his face bright red.

"I'm warning you, Masterson," he finally said, "somebody is going to end up dead."

"I've got no desire to kill one of your boys, Dan—" I began, but he turned on me viciously, cutting me off.

"You already done that once, ain't you, Adams? Why should it bother you to do it again?"

"I don't want to kill anyone, Dan," I told him steadily. "But if you don't keep Dell on a tight rein, it just might happen. I'm warning both of you."

"You dirty—" Dell began, but before he could reach for his gun old Dan grabbed his gun arm and said, "Let's go."

"But, Pa—"

"You mind me, boy!" Dan Curry shouted, pushing Dell towards the door. "Move!"

Dell backed out, staring at me murderously until his pa finally shoved him out the front door to the street.

"The old man knows you can take him," Bat said, turning towards me.

"Maybe," I said, hitching my chair closer to the table again.

"That's at least twice he's kept Dell from drawing his gun," Bat said. "You would have killed him either time."

"Maybe," I said again. "Dan just might want to

avoid trouble," I added thoughtfully, "which is a good reason to believe that he had nothing to do with the accidents."

"Well, there haven't been any more accidents," Bat pointed out, "which just might have something to do with the fact that you're here and a lot of people know who you are."

"Maybe," I said for a third time.

"Well, I'm sure as hell satisfied," Bat said. "Now all I need is a good poker game."

Right then, it would have taken a lot more than a good poker game to satisfy me.

The thought occurred to me just then that if Dell Curry were to show up dead all of a sudden, here was a whole room full of people who had heard me talk about killing him.

I guess there's a little prophet in us all.

TWENTY-THREE

I was awakened the next morning by someone's insistent banging on my door.

"What?" I called out.

"Come on, Clint, open up. It's Bat."

I staggered to my feet and opened the door.

"What time is it?"

"Never mind that," he said, closing the door behind him. "Dell Curry is dead."

I stared at him, then sat down on the bed.

"He was found this morning, in the barn at that old ranch the Currys are using. His head had been split open."

"With what?"

"Who knows? They got his body over at the mortician. Dan and his boys brought him in this morning. He's been yelling at the sheriff that you killed his boy."

I sat there, shaking my head.

"What are you thinking?" he asked.

"I'm wondering if Dell was really the intended victim," I said.

"What do you mean?"

"What if this was supposed to be another accident, only it was supposed to happen to Don Curry?"

"Jesus!" he said. "I hadn't thought of that."

"Does the sheriff want to see me?"

"I don't know that he wants to see you," Bat said wryly, "but he asked me to come over and *ask* you to come to his office."

"Well, then, we'd better get on over there and get this thing straightened out."

"You've got an alibi, if you want it," he said.

"What do you mean?" I asked, getting dressed.

"I'm talking about Lainie," he said. "She'd swear that she was with you all night if we wanted her to."

I stopped and just stared at him for a few seconds.

"Bat, do you think I killed him?"

"No, of course not," he assured me, "but if you want to avoid some trouble—"

"I don't need a phony alibi," I told him, and he remained silent while I finished dressing.

"Let's go," I said, strapping on my gun.

We walked across the street to the sheriff's office together, and a few people stopped and stared along the way.

"Story's gotten around," I commented.

"The Currys haven't exactly been quiet about it," he said.

When we walked into the sheriff's office I expected to find Dan Curry and his boys there, but the room was empty except for the portly little man seated behind the desk.

"Sheriff?" I asked, and damned if he didn't jump at the sound of my voice.

"Uh, y-yes, that's right."

How did this quivering tub of lard get to be sheriff, I wondered.

"I understand you want to talk to me. I'm Clint Adams."

"Uh, yes sir. A pleasure to meet you," he said, standing up. He was all of five-foot-seven or so, and the fear in his eyes was as plain as day. I had worn a star on my chest long enough to be offended by the fact that there was one on his, now.

"About the death of Dell Curry," I said.

"That's right. I, uh, it's my job to, uh—"

"Damn it, man!" I snapped. "Stopped shaking and stuttering and ask me the questions you're supposed to ask me. Where was I last night. In bed! Did I threaten to kill Dell Curry? No, I merely mentioned that I would not want to! Did I have a fight with him? Yes, but it was his choice! Did I kill him. No."

"I, uh, guess that's it, then," he said. "If you say you didn't do it . . ."

"How did you get to be sheriff, anyway?" I demanded, remembering all of the good men who had died standing up for what that badge represented.

Sheriff Tyler appeared to be at a complete loss for words, not knowing what to say—or afraid to say anything.

I turned to Bat and said, "Is there someone else we can talk to about this?"

Bat thought a moment, then said, "The mayor, I guess."

"Let's go."

Tyler started to stammer something then, but we both ignored him and left.

I must have been fuming because Bat said, "Don't get so upset just because the man was afraid of you."

"I'm not upset because he was afraid of me," I answered. "I'm upset because he's incompetent. How did he get that job?"

"The way people usually get jobs like that," Bat said. "Nobody else wanted it."

"Is the mayor the same way?"

"He might be intimidated by your reputation," Bat said. "But I don't think he'll be terrified of you."

"Well, good. I want this thing settled for the right reasons, not because some jelly-spined sheriff is too afraid to ask me the right questions."

"I don't see what you're upset about. Whatever the reason, the sheriff obviously has no intentions of conducting any kind of an investigation into Dell Curry's death."

"And how do you think Dan Curry is going to react to that?" I asked him.

"Whatever Dan Curry is going to do, he'll do," Bat said. "He doesn't strike me as the kind of man who would leave the matter in the hands of the law. Especially since you were a lawman when you killed his boy."

I followed Bat into the City Hall building where he told the Mayor's secretary who we were. She announced us to his honor, and we were escorted into his office.

"Masterson," the mayor said by way of greeting. He turned to me and said, "You're Clint Adams?"

"That's right."

He stared at me for a long moment, and I could see that Bat had been right. He wasn't afraid of me, but he was intimidated. He seemed determined not to let it show.

He turned back to Bat and said, "I'd like you gentlemen to give me a good reason why I should let this boxing tournament continue."

"Why shouldn't you?" I asked, before Bat had a chance to answer.

"A man is dead—" the mayor began, but I cut him off.

"Was he a contestant in the matches?"

"Well, no—"

"Then why should his death have any bearing on whether or not the matches should go on as planned?"

"His brother is a contestant," the mayor said.

"That doesn't mean that his death was connected in any way with our tournament," Bat spoke up.

The mayor dry-washed his hands as if trying to decide whether to say what he was going to say, and then he went ahead and said it.

"The talk around town is that you threatened to kill Dell Curry last night," he said to me.

"As usual, the talk around town is wrong," I said.

He waited to see if I would explain, and when I didn't, he asked, "What do you mean?"

"You've got a room full of witnesses," I pointed out, "of which Bat here was one. Ask them what my exact words were. I said that I didn't want to *have* to kill Dell Curry. In fact, I think I said that I didn't want to kill anyone."

Holman looked at Bat, who said, "That's right, mayor."

"I don't see how you can use the death of Dell Curry to call off the fights," I said. "In fact, I think you'd even have a hard time convincing Dan that they should be called off."

"I want to know who killed Dell Curry," the mayor said.

"That's what your sheriff is for," I pointed out.

"That fat fool," Holman said in disgust.

"Then replace him."

"No one wants the job. As soon as I find someone, I will replace him."

"Fine, then you can have that man investigate Dell Curry's death," I said, standing up. "I was up in my room all night. I'll make a statement to that effect."

The mayor stood up and said, "Wait, please."

I had started for the door and now I stopped. Bat hadn't moved, as if he had expected the mayor to call me back.

"Yes?"

"You were a lawman once, Mr. Adams," Holman said. "Could I persuade you—"

"To put on Tyler's badge?" I finished for him. "I wouldn't touch that tin star with a fishing pole."

"Mr. Adams, I need someone in the sheriff's office who can do the job."

"Then raise the salary. Maybe you'll get some takers then. I'm out of the law-and-order business."

I started for the door and he called out, "Wait," again. I looked at Bat, who hadn't moved, and he looked at the ceiling.

"Mr. Mayor, if you've got something to say, then say it," I said, still looking at Bat.

"Could I persuade you—that is, could I hire you, er, privately, to look into the death of Dell Curry, as well as the injuries to the three other men?"

"Why not just shut down the competition, Mr. Mayor, as you've threatened to do?"

"I can't," he said, dejectedly. "The town needs the revenue that the boxing matches will generate."

"And if you did shut it down, and the town lost out on that revenue, you wouldn't get reelected, would you?"

He looked down at the desk top and said, "No, I wouldn't."

"Who would pay me if I agreed?" I asked.

"The town council has agreed that each member would chip in a certain amount for your fee."

"What's your offer?"

"Two-hundred dollars, and another two when you find the guilty party."

I hesitated long enough for him to think I was going to accept, then said, "Forget it," and started for the door. "Come on, Bat."

Bat finally moved, and when the mayor called out, "Wait," for the third time, we both turned.

"Mr. Mayor, part of my responsibility as co-promoter of this tournament is to find out who caused those accidents and to make sure that no more happen. If I should find out who killed Dell Curry along the way, I'll let you know."

I walked out, and Bat followed.

"I don't understand you," he said out on the street. "You just turned down four-hundred dollars to do something you were going to do, anyway."

"That's the point," I said, wondering if he was too young to understand. "I'm not for sale, Bat. That's all there is to it. He was going to buy me, and by doing so buy himself into another term as mayor."

"But four-hundred dollars—"

"I'll tell you what," I said, stopping in my tracks. "You go back in there and tell him that you'll take the job."

"Me?" he said. "You should have seen the look on his face when I first went into his office and told him I wanted to promote a boxing tournament in his town. He's got this problem with my age, you know?"

"So do I, sometimes," I said, frankly, but he took the remark well, aware of the fact that I wasn't quite myself that morning.

"You need a drink," he said, "and a chance to calm down."

"I need a pot of good strong coffee," I corrected him, "but you're right about needing a chance to calm down."

Meeting Sheriff Tyler had bothered me more than it should have, and meeting the mayor on top of that hadn't helped. I led Bat to the café, where I ordered a pot of coffee, sat back and tried to relax myself.

I couldn't relax fully, though, not until I knew how Dan Curry was going to react to the death of his second son, twelve years after the death of his oldest.

Would he just assume that I was responsible, or would he wait for proof? And if he did assume I had killed him, would he come after me right away, or wait until after the boxing matches had been held?

Sure, I thought, pouring my first cup of hot coffee, go ahead and relax.

TWENTY-FOUR

After two pots of coffee, I told Bat that I wanted to go over to the undertaker's to see Dell Curry.

"What the hell for?"

"I want to know exactly how he died," I explained.

"Okay, but don't blame me if we run into Dan Curry and his other sons there."

"We won't," I said.

I was sure Dan Curry wouldn't be there. He wasn't the type of man to stand over his boy's body, grieving openly. I knew that for a fact. He'd done it with Dan Jr., and he'd do it with Dell, now. They were gone, there was no sense mooning over their bodies.

Bat walked me over to the undertaker, then told me he had some work to do and would see me later.

"Got to get the matches set up so we can start on time," he said. The first matches were only a couple of days away, so I told him to go ahead and do what he had to do.

97

"Yeah," he replied, "you too, but don't get killed doing it, all right?"

"Count on it, partner," I said.

I went in and met the undertaker, a man named Walter Dunn.

"What can I help you with, mister?"

"I'd like to see the body of Dell Curry, if that's possible," I said.

"Sure it's possible," he said. "I ain't done nothing to it, yet. Just got it this morning." He peered at me suspiciously and asked, "You like looking at bodies, do you?"

"Just this one," I answered.

"I mean, I got me a body in the back would knock your socks off, you know? Nice young girl, only fourteen—"

I stared at him hard and said, "Just show me Curry, and then shut your mouth, okay?"

"Well, sure," he said, blinking. "No need to get snappish about it. This way."

He took me into his back room and showed me where Dell Curry was laid out.

"What killed him?" I asked, looking at the back of his head, which looked as if it had been split wide open with an axe.

"Durned if I know," he answered. "I ain't no doctor."

"Where is the doctor?"

" 'Cross the street."

"Did he look at him?"

"He did."

"What's the doctor's name?"

"Doc Gilman, right across the way."

"Thanks."

I left him mumbling to himself about ungrateful people snapping at people who were just trying to be sociable.

As advertised, Doc Gilman's office was right across the street, above the barbershop. I wondered if the doctor doubled as the barber, which wouldn't give me all that much faith in his abilities as a physician.

I walked around to the side of the building and ascended the stairs to the doctor's office. When I knocked, the door was opened by a young girl of about eighteen, with long brown hair and big, round brown eyes. She was wearing a dress, and the body underneath was slim, with just a hint of small, round breasts.

"Now, you can't be the doctor," I said to her. Seeing that pretty young thing standing there with a startled, innocent expression in her eyes had improved my mood immediately. Nothing like a pretty girl to make things look better.

"My father is the doctor," she said. "He's not in right now. Can I help you?"

"Are you a doctor, too?" I asked.

"No, not really. I've learned some from my father. He says I'd make a good nurse. Is there something I can help you with?"

I was tempted to string her along, just to get her to check me out a little, but decided against it.

"Did the doctor look at the body of the man who was brought in this morning?" I asked.

"Oh, yes. Curry was the name, wasn't it?" she asked.

"That's right."

"I'm sure he did, Mister . . ."

"Adams, Clint Adams. And your name?"

"Melody Gilman. Would you like to come in and wait for him?" she asked, stepping back.

"Will he be long?"

"Not very. He's gone to check on Mrs. Withers. She's with child and due soon. He should be back directly."

"Well, then," I said, removing my hat and stepping forward, "if it's no trouble, I'll wait."

"It's no trouble at all," she said, closing the door behind us. "I was just cleaning up some. Can I get you something to drink while you wait? Coffee, or something stronger?"

"Coffee would be fine, if you have it made," I said.

"I'll just be a moment," she assured me, and walked through a curtained doorway which I assumed led to a kitchen.

She was quite different from either Lainie Bolt or Maggie Harris. Lainie's charms were obvious, even flagrant, while Maggie's were bold, challenging. Melody Gilman was . . . quietly lovely. It worked on you kind of easy like, instead of leaping out and grabbing you by the throat.

She came back carrying a cup of hot coffee, saying, "I hope I wasn't too long."

"You weren't long at all," I assured her, taking the cup. I tasted the coffee and it was delicious. I told her so.

"I thank you. I can't cook worth a lick, but I pride myself on making a good cup of coffee."

"That you do," I said. "Don't let me keep you from your work."

"Oh, you're not," she said. "I was just cleaning the place up—again—to break the boredom. I welcome having someone to talk to," she said, frankly.

"Well, I welcome having someone as lovely as you to talk to," I replied, and she blushed just a bit.

"Why are you interested in this man Curry?" she asked.

I wondered how much to tell her, then decided to tell her the truth—as far as it went.

I explained that I was co-promoting the boxing matches, and that the dead man's brother was involved. I told her about the accidents—which she said she knew about—and that I was wondering if this incident wasn't connected with the others.

"They you're trying to find out who killed the man?" she asked excitedly. "Like a detective?"

"Something like that, yes," I said, putting down the now empty coffee cup.

"That sounds very exciting."

I was about to tell her that it wasn't when the door opened and a big man carrying a black bag walked in. He stopped short and stared at us, and if he were her husband instead of her father, the look on his face might have worried me. He was well over six feet tall, with dark hair and a dark, handlebar mustache.

"What's this?" he demanded in a deep bass.

"Oh, Father," Melody said, rising from her

chair and rushing to his side. "This is Clint Adams. He wanted to talk to you about that man you examined this morning. He's trying to find out who killed him."

"Is that so?" he asked, looking at her. "Well, Mr. Adams, from what I've heard, you should be your own number one suspect."

"Father!" she said, in a scolding tone.

"Go for a walk, Melody," he said.

"Father, why—"

"I said go for a walk," he said again. "Do as you're told. I don't want any daughter of mine consorting with a known gunman."

"Doctor Gilman—"

He pointed a finger at me and said, "I'll speak with you, Adams, but not until my daughter leaves the room."

Melody looked at me with wide eyes, then quietly went and got a shawl and left the room. Her father continued to stare at me with a malevolence I felt I did not deserve, especially from a man I had never seen before.

TWENTY-FIVE

"You mind telling me what all of that was about?" I asked.

"Ask your questions and get out," was all he answered.

"Doctor, I don't understand why you have this animosity towards me. I assure you, to the best of my knowledge it is undeserved."

"You make your living with a gun, Adams," he said to me. "I have always despised men who make their living killing other people."

"I don't know where you got this idea—"

"Do you deny that you are called 'The Gunsmith'?" he asked.

"No, I don't deny it, but neither do I have to explain it to you, nor do I have to defend myself from—"

"Then it's settled," he said abruptly. "Ask your questions and then please leave my home. I have the right to make these demands of you."

"It's your home," I said, "and you do have the right. I would like to know what killed Dell Curry."

"A blow to the back of the head with an as yet unidentified instrument."

"An accidental blow?"

"It's impossible for me to answer that question with any degree of certainty," he said. He was answering my questions precisely, adding nothing more.

"Do you have any guesses as to what the instrument might have been?" I asked.

"None."

"Doctor, you are not being very helpful," I said, starting to feel impatient.

"I am answering your questions," he replied. "That is all I agreed to do. Now, if you've finished—"

"I'm finished," I said, interrupting him. I walked past him to the door, putting my hat back on. "Something may be on your mind, doctor, but I don't appreciate your taking it out on me. The next time you do, I'll take it as a direct insult."

He glared back at me, not at all intimidated by the "known gunman." I held back the other things I would have liked to have said to him and left.

At the bottom of the stairs I was met by Melody Gilman.

"Are you really the one they call 'The Gunsmith'?" she asked.

"Not you, too," I said.

"I'm sorry," she said. "I'm sorry for the way my father treated you, but you have to understand—"

"I understand that your father is rude, pig-headed—"

"He has a right," she said, interrupting me.

"Five years ago there was a gunfight out in the street, and my mother was killed by a stray bullet. Since then he's hated guns and, even more, men who made their living with guns."

"I sympathize," I said, "but with you more than him. I don't know where he got his information, Melody, but I am not a gunman. I have a certain reputation as a lawman, and there were times when I had to use my gun to uphold the law. If that's making my living with a gun—"

She touched my arm and said, "I understand . . . Clint. Can I call you Clint?"

"Of course."

"I'm sorry my father took out his grief on you. I'm sure you don't deserve it."

"Thank you, Melody."

"I have to go back in now," she said, putting one foot on the first step. "Perhaps we'll see each other again?"

I smiled at her and said, "I'd bet on it, Melody."

TWENTY-SIX

Walking back to my hotel, I found that I was the center of attention. Everyone I passed stared at me, and followed me as I walked along. I could feel their eyes on my back.

So Dan Curry had made his move, and it was an unexpected one. He was spreading my fame as a "known gunman." He had probably told the story of how I had killed his first son, and was now saying that I had killed his second. He was making the townspeople suspect me, and perhaps inciting some of them to take some action against me, so that he wouldn't have to.

I checked Bat's room and found him in. I explained what I thought Curry had been up to, and added the doctor's reaction to me as more proof.

"He's got a devious mind, that old man," Bat commented.

"That he does," I replied. "Is there anyone in this town who might take his bait?"

"Not that I've met while I've been here," he said, "but what if he puts a price on your head?"

106

"With what? As long as I've known the Currys, they've never had a lot of money. I don't think we have to worry about that."

"We?" he asked. "You mean *you*, don't you? Nobody's after me. Maybe you should pack up and ride out, Clint. That might be healthier for you."

"Is that what you want me to do?" I asked.

"You know me better than that, Clint," Bat said.

"And you know me better, as well," I replied.

"I just wanted you to know that I would understand," Bat told me.

"What will you do now that the doctor has proven no help?" Bat asked.

"I'm going to assume that Dell's death is another accident that went one step too far."

"You think it was meant for Don Curry instead?"

"I'm going to go on that assumption, but we'll keep that decision between you and me."

"Why? I think we established that any threat by the mayor to call the whole thing off would be just so much hot air."

"Let's not throw it in his face, though. We'll keep it between us."

"Okay, we'll do it your way."

I looked at the piece of paper he was writing on, and saw that he was matching up names for the first contests.

"How are you deciding who will fight who?"

He gave me a sly look and said, "Just between you and me?"

I smiled and said, "Yeah."

"The contestants have been told that I would draw lots to see who met who in the first round, but I'm matching them up so that the better fighters will still be around for the second round."

"You mean, you're not letting the better fighters meet each other too early?"

"Right. All we need is for the good ones to knock each other off and then we end up with a plowboy going up against Mike McCoole. We'd be a laughingstock. I want someone who is at least going to last a few rounds with the champ."

"Speaking of lasting a few rounds, do you know if Maggie got Jed Hunt to agree to spar with Billy?"

"I believe she did," he answered. "I think today is going to be their first session."

"I'd like to see that."

"What happened between the two of you the other night?"

"What do you mean?"

"She acted very strangely when I mentioned your name, and so did Billy."

"I'll have to talk to them."

"You're not going to tell me, are you?" he asked.

"Do I ask you what you do with little Bonnie Mapes—who I haven't met yet, by the way."

"That's it, turn the tables. I'll let you meet Bonnie, because I don't think you're any threat to me. I don't think she likes older men."

"I'll see you later," I said, and he laughed as I walked out.

TWENTY-SEVEN

I went over to the livery stable and I was just in time to watch Billy square off with big Jed. It was a frightening scene. Just looking at them, you couldn't help but believe that someone was going to end up getting hurt, or killed.

Maggie was standing off to one side, calling out encouragement and instructions to her younger brother.

"He's a lot bigger than you, Billy, but that won't bother you none. Don't be afraid to hit him, he can take it," she was telling him.

None of the three of them were aware of my presence as Billy and Jed raised their fists and advanced on each other. I didn't know what kind of a deal they had made with Jed, but this session would tell him whether or not he had a chance in the tournament.

I watched as Billy flicked out his left jab a couple of times, catching Jed on the face, but the big man did not seem to be fazed by it. He just shook his head and kept moving in with his big fists held out in front of him. He seemed content to let Billy jab at his face without mounting any kind of offense of his own. Maggie was yelling at both of them now to start punching, but they moved around that way for the next few moments, Billy reaching out with his jab, and Jed shaking them off.

"The body, Billy, hit him in the body," Maggie called out.

Obeying her, he dug a couple of half-hearted digs to the body, which did not effect Jed Hunt at all.

I didn't think either man was learning very much from this, and Maggie seemed to agree. She was almost frantic on the sidelines, shouting at Billy to get to work.

Finally, Jed decided to throw a punch, a long, lazy overhand right that caught Billy by surprise. That fist must have been like a club, and Billy staggered back from the blow, his face showing his surprise.

Maggie howled and I waited for Billy to fall, but to his credit he gathered himself together and avoided Jed's next blow.

Then he went to work.

He threw two jabs at Jed's face, harder, more stinging jabs than he had previously thrown, and as Jed blinked, he threw a hard right that caught the big man flush on the nose. Blood spurted, but Billy didn't stop. Jed remained on his feet, so Billy threw two more jabs, and then another right, sending Jed back a few more feet. Billy repeated the process again and again, driving Jed all the way across the corral, but the big man refused to fall down. He was blinded by blood from cuts over his eyes, and his hands were down low. He was defenseless, and Billy continued to pummel him. I knew I had to step in before Jed was seriously injured.

"That's enough!" I shouted, moving forward on the run. Maggie heard me, but Billy did not. He continued to hit Jed until I entered the corral, grabbed him around the waist and pulled him away from the defenseless man. I spun Billy around and positioned myself in front of Jed, who was breathing raggedly. Billy turned back around and was about to throw another punch when he saw that it was me in front of him and not his opponent.

I thought he was going to throw that punch, anyway.

"Do you want to fight me, Billy?" I asked him, balling up my fists just in case he did. I didn't think I'd fare any better than Jed did, but I certainly would not have stood there and let him hit me at will.

The look on his face was oddly cold and distant, and before we could discover whether or not he did want to fight me, Maggie stepped between us.

"Billy, no!"

She hung on his arms and pushed against him, trying to get him to back up. Behind me I could hear Jed trying to breath through a nose that must have been broken, and knew that we had to get him to a doctor.

Maggie kept talking to Billy, and gradually the cold look faded from his eyes and they became as guileless as ever.

"Maggie?" he said.

She turned towards me and said, "It's all right now, Clint."

I turned and looked at Jed Hunt's battered and bloody face. He seemed to be out on his feet, unaware of what was going on around him.

"Maggie, we have to get him to the doctor," I said.

"I've hurt him," I heard Billy say. I turned and saw that Billy was looking at Jed with great concern on his face.

"Billy, walk him to the doctor. It's over the barbershop."

"I know where," he said, coming forward. He took one of Jed's arms and put it around his neck, so he could support the big man.

As they staggered away I turned to Maggie and said, "I thought you said that he didn't like to hurt people?"

She was staring after them also and answered by saying, "Not now, Clint. I better go with him."

"Maggie—" I said, grabbing her arm to keep her from running after them.

She gave me a hard look and pulled her arm free.

"I said not now!"

"Well, we've got to talk sometime," I told her firmly.

She backed off and said, "All right, I'll talk to you later, after I've seen to Billy."

"Seen to Billy?" I said. "He's not the one who needs to be seen to, Maggie. Did you see what he did to Hunt? And he enjoyed it."

"Clint, please," she said, putting her hands on my arms. "Please," she said again, then turned and hurried after her brother and the man he'd nearly killed during a sparring session.

TWENTY-EIGHT

"I thought you told me that he didn't like to hurt people in the ring," Bat said after I'd explained to him what happened.

"That's what Maggie told me, but after what I saw, I don't know."

"He really took the big fella apart, huh?"

"He was methodical, Bat. And he had this funny look in his eyes. When I stepped between them he didn't recognize me right away. I thought he was going to hit me, too."

"And that only started after Jed Hunt had hit him?"

"Yeah. Before that he seemed to just be playing with him."

"Like he didn't want to hurt him?"

"Yeah, and then all of a sudden—pow! the kid went off like a stick of dynamite."

"I guess I'll have to watch him close during the bouts," Bat said.

"Who is going to referee the fights?" I asked.

"Oh, didn't I tell you?" he asked, smiling.

"Tell me what?" I asked, suspiciously.

"We are."

I stared at him. "Great. I'll have to make sure I wear my gun."

"You won't have to do much," Bat explained. "Just make sure they fight each other instead of dance with each other. We don't want the paying customers to get restless."

"Sure. Where's the ring going to be set up?"

"There's a clearing just north of town. We'll be set up there. In fact, they should be putting it up today. I'll have to get over there and make sure they get it right."

"You know all about building a boxing ring, right?"

He stood up and said, "I know many things, Mr. Adams. See you later."

We were in the café having coffee and I watched him walk out and then ordered another pot. Thirty seconds later I canceled the order. I decided to go over to the saloon instead and have a few drinks with Iron Ben Neal.

I thought I had finally come up with a job for him.

TWENTY-NINE

"Referee?" Ben Neal asked, mouth agape. "You want me to be a referee?"

"Bat and I are a little inexperienced in that aspect of the game, Ben. We could use someone with your know-how. How about it? Can you handle it?"

I could just see this little man getting in between two giants and breaking them up, but I still thought he had a better chance of doing it—without a gun—than I did.

"Sure I can handle it, Clint! I can handle it just fine." He looked down at the top of the bar and seemed to sneer at it. "Back in the ring," he said, only half-aloud.

"Before you get back in the ring, Ben, do you think you could get me a beer?"

"Sure, sure," he said, hurrying away with new spring in his step.

When he came back with the beer I said, "Now, we can't afford to pay you all that much—"

"Pay me? Clint, you're giving me a chance to get back inside the ring. For that you don't have to pay me."

I put my hand on his shoulder and picked up my beer with the other hand, saying, "We'll work something out, Ben. Okay?"

"Sure," he said for maybe the hundredth time.

I patted his shoulder and then walked to an empty corner table.

I sat and finished my beer, debated about whether or not to have another, then decided to walk over to the doctor's office and check on Jed Hunt's condition. If the doctor would even talk to me, that is.

Melody must have seen me from a window, because as I approached the steps leading up to her father's office, the door opened and she came rushing down.

"I don't think you should go in there, Clint," she said, grabbing hold of one of my arms.

"Why not?"

"They're all still in there. The man who was hurt, and the other boy with his sister. Father's in a foul mood, because he's against men fighting each other for sport."

"What isn't your father against?" I asked.

"We can't talk here," she said. "Let's go for a walk."

She slipped her arm through mine and we started walking. I could smell the clean scent of her hair and the equally clean fresh scent of her.

"My father is not a bad man," she said in defense of him.

"I didn't mean to imply that he was," I told her. "He's got a lot of hate inside of him, though. It seems to be eating away at him."

"That's true. Let's walk out there," she said, pointing away from town. "Less chance of anyone seeing us and telling father."

"Why are you worried about that?"

"He told me to stay away from you."

"You're a grown woman, Melody. Who you see should be your business."

"Tell that to my father," she said.

"Your father doesn't want to hear much of anything from me," I reminded her. "How's Jed Hunt?"

"He was pretty dazed when they brought him up. He's got some nasty cuts above his eyes. Father wants to observe him for a while to see if he's got a concussion. If he doesn't, he should be fine." She bent over to pick up a small, round stone and, weighing it in her hand, said, "I guess that's one point on which my father and I agree."

"Which point?"

"On fighting. I can't understand why two grown men would want to beat each other with their fists for sport."

"I can think of something better for two grown people to do," I said. She looked at me sharply and I added, "A man and a woman, I mean."

Her look turned shy and she looked away, trying to find a good place to throw that round little stone.

"Why did you come out to meet me?" I asked.

"I wanted to keep you and father apart. I don't think you need each other's abuse."

"Watching out for both of us, huh?" I asked.

"Yes, I guess. . . ."

She finally picked out a good place and heaved the stone. We both watched it land and then she turned and looked at me. We had walked far enough that we could not be seen from town.

"You're shy," I said.

"Yes," she admitted, "but right now I wish I wasn't."

I put my hands gently on her shoulders and said, "I'm not shy at all."

I pulled her to me and she came willingly, mouth open and eager. Her shyness faded away in the face of unbridled, young passion as she clutched at me and rubbed herself against me as if she were trying to get underneath my skin. It was the closest I had ever come to having sex while I was still dressed.

She broke away breathlessly and said, "I've wanted to do that ever since . . . since I first saw you."

I pointed my index finger at her face and said, "Now that's not a very shy thing to say."

She dropped her eyes and said, "I'm shy, but I'm trying to overcome it. Clint," she went on, meeting my eyes with a very bold, totally unshy gaze, "can we be . . . together?"

I knew what she meant and debated pretending that I didn't, but I didn't want her to think I was laughing at her, or making fun of her.

Besides that, being "together" with this lovely young girl appealed to me very much.

"What about your father?" I asked.

"He doesn't have to know."

"Where?" I asked.

She smiled and said, "We'll find a place. I have to get back, now."

"How will we keep in touch?" I asked, wondering if she had it all planned out in her lovely little head.

"I've got it all planned," she said, like a mindreader, and then she kissed me shortly and ran off.

THIRTY

When I got back to my hotel I was hoping to find Maggie waiting there to talk to me, but I was disappointed. Not only wasn't she there, but I had the feeling that she might even try to avoid me, and thereby avoid the subject of what had happened that afternoon. On an off-chance I checked the desk for messages, but there were none.

I decided to go looking for her.

She wasn't at the boardinghouse, and neither was Billy. Likewise, they hadn't gone back behind the livery stable to continue his training session. I checked the livery and found that a buckboard had been rented.

Had they run out? I didn't think so. Maybe they went for a long ride so she could talk to her brother without being interrupted. Maybe when they came back, she'd come to me to talk, also. I decided to wait for their return, instead of saddling Duke up and going out after them. Maggie wanted that title much too much to run out because Billy had badly beaten Jed Hunt while sparring.

Walking back towards my hotel I spotted Dan Curry standing across the street, watching the front door. Maybe he was waiting for me to come out, so I figured I'd walk over and surprise him.

"Hello, Dan," I said from his blind side. He was angled to his left and I came up on his right. When he heard my voice he started and stared at me in surprise, but his look quickly turned to one of hatred.

"What do you want, Adams?" he demanded.

"Well, I was kind of going to ask you the same thing, Dan," I said, "seeing as how you're watching my hotel. You looking for somebody in particular?"

"I'm just standing on the street, Adams. Is there any law against that?"

"Not that I know of," I said.

"Then why don't you just leave me be? You don't know how much willpower it's taking me not to draw on you."

"Guess you're not in that much of a hurry to die, huh Dan?" I said. "See you around."

To my retreating back he said, "I ain't forgot about my boys, Adams. Don't think I forgot about my boys."

I ignored him and kept walking to my hotel.

Since Bat had woken me up before I was ready, I figured I'd go on up and relax some and try to sort some things out. When I got up to my floor I thought I heard footsteps hurrying down the hall. I turned the corner in time to see a man disappear down the back steps.

"Hey!" I shouted. I started out after him but

even before I got to the steps I heard the back door slam. He'd be long gone by the time I got outside. I stopped short and walked back to my room, wondering which room the man had come out of and why he was in such an all-fired hurry to get out of the building.

Before opening my door I pulled my gun and then pushed the door open slowly. I entered with my gun held out in front of me, but relaxed when it became obvious that the room was empty. I put my gun away and shut the door behind me. It was all too curious, Curry out in front of the hotel, and some unknown man—one of his sons?—inside and on my floor. Something had to be wrong.

I looked around some more but couldn't find anything out of place. A check out the front window showed that Dan Curry had gone.

I was about to take off my gun when I thought I caught some kind of movement in the room. I looked around again, though, and didn't see anything. I hadn't really *seen* anything move, it was just that I'd felt, or maybe caught something out of the corner of my eye.

I stood stock still and waited and then I saw it again.

It was the bed. Something was moving beneath the covers on the bed. I walked to the bed and, with my gun in my right hand, I grabbed the blanket with my left and yanked it off.

I heard the rattler before I saw it and I fired from pure reflex. I caught the ugly creature in mid-strike and just about blew his head off. A split second slower and I'd have been snake-bit.

Holstering my gun I looked for something to put the snake in and came up with a small sack someone had left in the room. Very handy.

I walked to the livery with the sack, saddled Duke, tied the sack to the saddle horn and then rode out. I took my time, because I didn't want to get to the ranch before Dan Curry did.

I wanted him to be there so I could throw that snake in his face.

THIRTY-ONE

I wasn't riding the main trail, which was probably the only reason I saw them. They were underneath a tall oak, well out of sight of the main road, and if their horses hadn't been making a racket, I might have ridden right up on them.

It was Maggie and Billy, with the buckboard they had rented, but they weren't alone. Billy was standing by the buckboard team, but Maggie was deep in heated conversation with a tall man who was dressed for the city. They looked like they were having much more than just a conversation, though. It looked like an argument. I had the feeling that the man was someone Maggie already knew. He made a move to touch her a couple of times; once she stood for it, the other time she pulled away. I just watched until they were finished. The man had the last word, spreading his hands in a helpless gesture, looking firm, but apologetic. Maggie stood there staring at him with her hands on her hips for a short spell and then without another word she stalked back to the buckboard. Billy helped her up and then got beside her and they headed for town. The man stayed there and looked after them for a few minutes, then he mounted up and rode toward town at a considerably slower pace.

I had not seen the man in town up to now, so I assumed that he had not been there until now. When I got back I'd look into who he was and what he wanted, but right now I had a prior appointment that I was eager to keep.

I knew that going to the Curry camp was risky, but I wanted Dan to know that his plan had failed. I hoped, however, that I would be able to ride in and ride out without having to kill anyone. I had enough Curry blood on my hands for a lifetime.

As I rode into their camp I saw Dan as I had seen him the last time I was there, leaning on the corral fence, watching his two boys spar. That was good. Neither of the boys was wearing a gun, so if push came to shove I'd only have old Dan to worry about.

He heard me and turned as I rode up on him. The look on his face told the whole story.

"Adams—" he started, but I threw the sack at him and it hit him in the chest, cutting him off.

"I believe that belongs to you, Dan," I told him.

He threw the sack down, not at all curious about what was in it because he obviously already knew.

"I ain't denying nothing, Adams, I'm just sorry as hell to see you up and around."

"I know you are, Dan," I said, "but I intend to be up and around for a long time. Remember that."

His hatred was choking him too much to allow

him to speak, and neither of his sons seemed inclined to speak as they watched us, so I backed Duke away from them, keeping an eye on Dan's gunhand the whole time. I didn't seriously think he'd go for his gun. As much as he hated me, he wasn't a fool. He knew he had no chance of getting to his gun before I got to mine. Nevertheless, I kept Duke backing away and kept a wary eye on the old man.

Drawing on me may have been beyond him, but shooting me in the back was not.

THIRTY-TWO

Riding back to town I thought again about the odd exchange I had witnessed between Maggie Harris and the stranger. What had that been about, and on top of that, who was the man?

I pushed Duke on a bit faster, wanting to get back to town and find out who the stranger was.

Finding out the man's name wasn't hard. After leaving Duke at the livery I went to my hotel and, sure enough, the man had registered. His only other choice would have been the boardinghouse, and with Maggie staying there, I doubted that he would.

All I had to do was describe the man to the clerk, and he told me that the man had registered just a short time ago. He showed me the register and I read the man's name: Roy Wagner. The address was from the East, which might explain where Maggie and he had met before.

"Did he say what he did for a living?" I asked the clerk, who was a perpetually bored looking little man with wire-frame glasses and a neck like a chicken.

"I didn't ask," he replied.

"Thanks," I said, returning the register, which had told me one other thing: Wagner's room was two doors from mine.

I decided to go over to the saloon and see if Wagner wouldn't show up there to wash away the trail dust.

I got a beer from Ben and explained to him that a stranger had ridden into town today and that I was interested in what he wanted here. I told him I'd appreciate it if he would talk to the man when he came in for a drink and see what he could find out.

"Sure, Clint. What's this fella's name?"

"Roy Wagner," I said.

"Wagner?" he asked, surprised. "Is he in town?"

"You know him?" I asked, equally surprised.

"I don't know him, but I know who he is. He's a writer for a newspaper back East. He writes about boxing."

"That's all he does, write about boxing?"

"And he gets paid for it," Neal said. "He usually follows the champ around."

"McCoole?"

"Or whoever the champ happens to be at the time."

"I see. So he's probably here because this is McCoole's next stop."

"We still got a little over a week before McCoole shows up," Neal said. "Long enough for us to hold our matches."

"Have you talked with Bat about getting paid to referee?" I asked him.

"No, I figured you'd pay me whatever you thought was fair."

"I'll take care of it, Ben," I promised. I picked up my beer and said, "If Wagner comes in, though, I'd like to meet him."

"I'll introduce you, don't worry."

I thanked him and went to my corner table. It would appear very natural for Ben to introduce me to Wagner, since I was co-promoter of the matches he was probably here to watch.

I was halfway through my beer when Wagner came walking into the saloon, still wearing his Eastern duds. I watched him closely as he went to the bar and saw Ben Neal immediately engage him in conversation. Before long Ben inclined his head towards me.

Wagner turned with a beer in his hand and came over to my table. He was a tall, thin man with a droopy mustache and a large nose, and he seemed to squint all the time.

"Mr. Adams?" he asked, reaching my table.

"That's right."

"My name is Roy Wagner, sir," he said, extending his hand to me.

"Mr. Wagner."

"May I sit down?"

"Depends on your business," I said.

"I'm a reporter from back East," he said. "I'm here about these boxing matches that you are co-promoting."

"In that case, have a seat," I told him.

"Thank you."

"Pardon me if I stare, sir, but I believe that I

recognize your name, and not in connection with boxing." He stopped talking and continued to stare.

I didn't offer to help him with his memory, because I was sure that he already knew who I was.

"Haven't you been called 'The Gunsmith'?" he asked finally.

"I have," I admitted. "Some over-ambitious newspaperman called me that years ago and it stuck."

"I'm rather pleased to find you here, sir, for two reasons," he said. "One, of course, is this tournament which will decide who will face Mike McCoole when he arrives, but the other reason is that I would dearly love to do a story on you."

"Not interested."

"Listen to my offer, sir. I could make you famous, a legend of the West—"

"Stop right there, mister," I said, cutting him off. "I don't particularly like being called 'The Gunsmith' as it is, so the last thing I want to do is become famous for it. No thank you."

"But you don't know what you're turning down—"

"If you'd like to talk about boxing, Mr. Wagner, I'd be only too happy to oblige. If not, I'd like to finish my beer in peace," I told him.

He began to protest, then thought better of it and remained silent.

"Very well," he said, finally. "I will drop the matter . . . for now. I warn you, though, I would not be very good at my job if I took no for an answer the first time."

I decided to respect him for that, until he made me feel otherwise.

"Fair, Mr. Wagner, but let's drop it for now."

"Done," he said. "May I buy you another beer?"

"Done," I mimicked, and he smiled and signaled Ben Neal for two more beers.

"Have you been following Mike McCoole on his entire trip?" I asked.

"Actually, I've been traveling ahead of him, not following him. I'm doing stories on the men that are waiting for him to arrive, rather than on the ones he's been leaving in his wake."

"Has he been doing well?" I asked.

"No one's been able to touch him, so far," he said. Ben came over with the beers and set them down without a word.

"I understand there are a few boys in this town who have high hopes," he added when Ben left.

"There are a couple who look good," I admitted, "but they're not from these parts."

"Is that a fact?" he asked. "What about the locals?"

"There's not much to recommend them," I said, honestly.

"What about these out-of-town boys, then?" he asked, and he had given me my opening to bring up Billy Harris's name and see how he reacted.

"Well, there's a kid name Don Curry," I began. "He's a big, strong kid and he looks pretty good."

A look of amusement came over Wagner's face as he listened to me comment on someone's boxing abilities. I could almost read his mind:

What would a gunfighter know about professional boxing? Still, he let me talk, obviously wanting to get on my good side so I would eventually agree to an interview.

"What about the other one?" he asked.

"Oh, that would be young Billy Harris," I said, innocently. "He's not as big as Curry, but I believe he's faster. Yeah, Billy has the edge in speed, but I think Curry likes to hit people more. Hey, Harris is from the East. Maybe you've heard of him, or his sister?"

"His sister?" Wagner said, showing no sign of recognition.

"Yeah, he's managed by his sister. Her name is Maggie, Maggie Harris. That ring a bell?" I asked.

He made a show of thinking it over, concentrating while he drank some of his beer. He shook his head as he put his mug down and said, "No, I can't say that either name rings a bell."

"Well, I guess the East is almost as big as the West, eh?" I commented. We laughed together, like good friends, and he signaled Ben for two more beers—on him, of course.

"Well, tell me, Mr. Adams—can I call you Clint?" he asked suddenly.

"Sure," I said.

"Good, and I wish you'd call me Roy."

"Fine with me," I said.

"Good!" he said, happy that we were fast becoming close friends. "Now then, Clint, would you agree to an interview, in your capacity as promoter of this tournament?"

"I don't think so, Roy."

"Now, what reason could you possibly have—"

"My partner, Bat Masterson," I said, interrupting, "put this whole thing together. I think that if you were to interview anyone, it should be Bat."

"Bat?" he asked. "That's a man's name?"

"That's Bat's name."

"Masterson?" he asked. I nodded and he took out a notebook and wrote something in it. "Who is this fellow?"

"Just a young fella who likes, uh, sports." When Bat played poker—the way he played poker, anyway—you really couldn't call it gambling, so maybe he was making poker into a sport.

"Young? How young?" Wagner asked.

"Oh, I guess Bat's about twenty-one, or thereabouts."

"Twenty-one?" he asked in surprise. "What's he know about boxing?"

I shrugged, saying, "I never asked him."

Wagner's mind was racing, and once again it didn't take much to figure out what he was thinking. A gunfighter and a kid! What do they know about boxing?

"Bat's a good organizer," I said.

"I certainly hope so," Wagner said, obviously not convinced.

"He should be in here fairly soon," I said. "I'll introduce you."

"Fine," he said without enthusiasm. "We might as well keep the beer coming," he added, signaling Ben.

"Is this how you writers prime yourselves?" I asked.

"This is where we pick up most of our information," he said, and the way he held up his empty mug, I wasn't sure if he meant in saloons, or in the beers.

"Well, let me get this one, then," I said, as Ben came over with the fresh mugs.

"Ben here was a fighter," I said, as Ben started to walk away. He turned at the sound of his name.

"Yes, he told me about his career," Wagner said.

"That's quite a record he has," I said.

"Which record is that?"

"Never having been knocked down."

"Oh, yes," Wagner said, looking at Ben, "quite a record, indeed."

Ben puffed up his chest and fairly strutted back to the bar.

"I saw him fight a few times," Wagner confided, when Ben was out of earshot. "They should have let him use his head, because he ignored his hands once he got inside the ring."

"What is it about him that kept him from being knocked down?" I asked out of real curiosity.

"That's an oddity," he said. "There have been a few men like Ben Neal who, no matter how hard or often they are hit, never seem to go down. Unfortunately, many of them keep going until they get killed in the ring. I guess Ben Neal showed a little more brains than most of them—although how anyone who would step into the ring could be said to have brains is beyond me."

He said that with such contempt that I had to comment on it.

"If you have such contempt for fighting, why do you write about it?"

He stared at me for a moment, then lifted his beer mug and said, "A few more of these, friend, and maybe I'll answer that question for you."

THIRTY-THREE

It took a little more than a few more, but Wagner finally told me why he wrote about boxing, even though he didn't like it.

For years he had been trying to get a job writing with a newspaper on a regular basis, but he had always been what he called a "stringer," selling his work wherever he could. Then one day Mr. Wagner got lucky and happened to be in the right place at the right time. He was in a saloon when a leading contender for a fight with the heavyweight champ got himself knocked out with one punch. Wagner grabbed hold of the man who knocked him out and did a story on him. For some reason, the story generated a lot of attention, and the end result was that the man—who had never fought before in a ring—got the title fight instead of the contender.

"That fight made me," he said, "but it killed that kid. He happened to get in a lucky punch in a saloon, but I had to be there to see it. He had a good chin, that kid, and he stood up to the champion for eleven rounds, but in the end when he went down, he never got up."

"And you blame yourself for that?" I asked.

He was about to say "yes" when he caught himself. I could virtually see him shake himself of the mood as he said, "I don't take the blame for anything. That kid never should have gotten into that ring, and it wasn't me who made him. I didn't hold a gun to his head."

I let the matter drop. Obviously, Wagner did blame himself for that kid's death, but he had to make a living.

There were a lot of us who didn't like the way we made a living. For years I had been a lawman, but when it got to the point where I wasn't enjoying what I was doing, because too many people were forcing me to enforce the law with my gun, I had quit and taken to the road. That was me, though. I couldn't condemn Wagner for not doing what I had done. He had to follow his own conscience.

If nothing else, I was impressed with the man's ability to drink beer and still keep a relatively clear head. I was about ready to stagger over to my hotel for a good night's sleep when Bat walked in, got himself a beer and joined us.

"Bat Masterson, Roy Wagner," I said as Bat sat down.

Wagner looked Bat over critically while Bat sat back and studied him curiously.

"Mr. Wagner is a sports reporter," I said, wondering if I'd gotten the man's title right. "He's here to watch our fights and then cover the fight with McCoole for some eastern newspapers."

"That's good," Bat said. "We can use the publicity."

"When is the first fight?" Wagner asked.

"Tomorrow, at noon. You'll get to see one of the better boys in action."

I didn't know how Bat had scheduled the fights, so I also didn't know who he was talking about.

"Clint told me you had a couple of promising boys," Wagner said. "Which one will we see tomorrow?"

"Curry," Bat said, looking at me. "Curry will be in the first fight. There will be five."

"Good."

"Mr. Wagner wants to interview you. I told him you were the organizer of the whole shooting match."

"Yes, if you have the time," Wagner said, taking out his notebook. He squinted and I thought perhaps he was doing so more than was normal, maybe due to the amount of beer he had drunk.

"Sure. Go ahead and ask away," Bat said.

"Before you gentlemen start," I said, rising, "I'm going to say goodnight."

"Be up early tomorrow," Bat told me. "That's when the action finally starts."

"Right. Good night, Roy."

"Good night, Clint. I'll see you at the fights."

As I walked to my hotel I was surprised to find that I was able to walk a pretty straight line. As I started up the stairs to my room, I reminded myself to check my bed for snakes, or any other little varmints.

When I got into my room there was somebody in my bed, all right, but it wasn't a varmint, and it wasn't anyone I would want to chase away.

It was Melody Gilman, and she smiled shyly as I lit the lamp and looked at her.

"Did you check for snakes?" I asked her.

"What?" she asked, frowning.

"Never mind. How did you get in?"

"The back door."

"What about your father?"

"He had to go out of town to deliver a baby," she said. "He will most likely be gone until tomorrow. Are you glad to see me?"

I was and I wasn't, but I told her I was. Maybe she sensed my reserve, because she lowered the blanket to show me that she was totally and invitingly naked.

She didn't have to ask me again if I was glad to see her.

THIRTY-FOUR

Her body was incredibly firm and taut all over. Her breasts were small, but her nipples were surprisingly large and I found myself fascinated by them. I sucked and bit them until she put her hand between us and grabbed my erection impatiently.

"Put it in me, please," she whispered.

I wondered for a fleeting moment if she was a virgin, and in fact I expected her to be, but I slid into her so easily that it was obvious that she was not. She knew what to do, too, because she wrapped her firm legs around my waist and dug her heels into my buttocks, fitting us as tightly together as possible. For a girl who was young and shy, she knew how she liked it, and I gave it to her the way she wanted it.

She started moving her little behind in a circular motion, and I matched her move for move as she increase her tempo. She was actually in control of the moment, and I found myself letting her have her head willingly.

Maybe I was too tired to argue, but not to tired to perform.

She began to moan louder and louder and buck underneath me. Her movements were so violent that she seemed to lose control of herself, and her legs dropped off my waist and flopped around on the bed as I let myself go and filled her up with my seed.

"Oh, God . . ." she moaned as I slid off of her, and I silently agreed with her.

As we lay side by side she looked over at me and said, "I guess you noticed that wasn't my first time."

"You don't have to explain anything to me," I assured her, wishing she wouldn't talk so I could go to sleep.

"I haven't done it a lot," she insisted, "just a few times."

"Mm, hmm," I said.

She ran her left hand over my chest and said, "It was never like this, though."

"Honey," I said, taking her hand, "if you think that was good just give me a few hours sleep and I'll show you what good really is."

It was an uncharacteristic boast on my part, but there was something about her youthful eagerness that made me want to match it. She stopped talking and I drifted off to sleep.

THIRTY-FIVE

She woke first in the morning and woke me up to make love again. She was energetic and I made good on my boast. So good, in fact, I was worried that Melody's sweet cries might rouse the desk clerk. I was getting the distinct impression, however, that I had been taken. She knew much too much for a girl who had "only done it a few times."

I shooed her out afterward, bathed and dressed, and ambled over to the café for breakfast. Roy Wagner and Bat were already eating and apparently still carrying on the interview that had started the night before.

"Good morning, gentlemen," I said, as I sat down. I told the waitress to bring me the same thing I'd had every day that I'd been in town, starting with a pot of good, strong coffee.

"Is this the same conversation I left last night?" I asked.

"It certainly is," Roy Wagner said, and he looked like a much happier man than I'd left the previous evening. His eyes were shining as he said, "Bat has been telling me some interesting stories."

"About boxing?"

"Hardly," Wagner said. "Bat has been telling me stories about a friend of his, Wyatt Earp, and about you, Clint."

"Roy wants to do some books on the three of us, Clint," Bat said, and I gave him a hard look which he either did not see or chose to ignore.

"Is that a fact?" I asked. "What about our boxing tournament?"

"Oh, we went over all of that last night," Wagner assured me.

"Well, I think that after breakfast Bat and I should go over and check out the set-up. Don't you think so, Bat?" I asked, giving him a shot in the shin with my boot.

That got his attention and he looked at me and said, "Yeah, I suppose so."

"I'll tag along if you don't mind," Roy Wagner said, and before I could comment Bat said, "Why sure, Roy. No problem."

"I see you two have become good friends."

"We understand each other," Wagner said to me.

By the time my breakfast came I had lost most of my appetite, so that by the time they were finished, I was ready to go, too.

"Why don't you go on ahead, Roy," I told Wagner. "I'd like to discuss something with Bat."

"What about my bill?" he asked, indicating the remnants of his breakfast.

"I'll take care of it. Go on."

He smiled widely and said, "Thanks. See you fellows later."

When he was gone and I'd paid for his breakfast as well as mine—I let Bat pay for his own—Bat said, "Buying his breakfast for him? What are you trying to do, get on his good side?"

"I don't want to get anywhere with him," I told him as we walked out. "Look, Bat, if you want to be a dime-novel hero, be my guest, but don't drag me into it."

"Huh? What's the matter with you?"

"The guy asked me for an interview last night and I said no. Now you start telling him stories about me."

"*Us,* about *us,*" he corrected me. "You, me and Wyatt. I told him about the time the three of us were holed up in that ghost town—"

"Just do me a favor," I interrupted him. "In the rest of your stories, leave me out."

"I guess you don't want to be famous," he said.

"I guess you're right," I answered. "I'm about as famous right now as I ever want to be."

As young as he was he obviously didn't understand my sentiments, but that was all right, as long as he kept his mouth shut about me from that point on.

"Who's refereeing this first fight?" I asked, changing the subject.

"Ben Neal. He's so pumped up I might let him do all of the bouts."

"It might be best for the fighters if he did," I commented. "What are we paying him?"

"Ten dollars a fight."

I was satisfied with that, and I was sure that Iron Ben Neal would be, too. I was very interested in seeing how Ben would do trying to control two men who were twice his size.

When we reached the fight area we could see that people were already clamoring for the fights to begin. Ben was collecting the money from the people who were willing to pay for a close-up position from which to watch the fight. Others were climbing trees and finding other places from which to watch the fight without paying. As Ben Neal put it, however, they wouldn't be able to "get sweat on" from out there.

Bat relieved Ben so that he could get ready to referee the first bout. I walked around, looking for Maggie Harris. According to Bat, Billy Harris wasn't fighting today, but I was sure that one or both of them would be there to watch the competition, especially Don Curry.

I spotted Maggie finally, but she didn't see me because she was watching Roy Wagner. Wagner was talking to Don Curry, who was standing outside the ring with his father and brother. I couldn't interpret the look on Maggie's face as she studied Roy Wagner. There was a hint of fear, and some distaste.

Eventually, Bat moved into the center of the ring to introduce the fighters. Curry was to fight a man named Oaks, who appeared to be about twenty-eight or so, but if he was a heavyweight, he barely made it; compared to Don Curry, he looked like a stringbean. They were the same height, but Curry had to have him by at least forty or fifty pounds.

After the introductions, Ben Neal came into the ring and signaled the fighters to begin.

Curry went right at Oaks, and for a while, Oaks held his own by staying out of harm's way. After three rounds of chasing Oaks, Curry was being yelled at in his corner by his old man, and when he came out for the fourth round, he began to stalk Oaks.

Up to this point he had been trying to knock Oaks out with one punch to the head, but now he closed on Oaks and threw a punch to the body. Oaks winced in pain because he didn't have enough meat on him to withstand a blow like that. He circled away throwing out a weak jab from time to time. Curry waded right through those jabs, however, and threw another body shot that almost folded Oaks in half. Curry was about to swing again, but he waited for Oaks to straighten up again and then hit him in the same spot, a hard right to the left side, and that was the end of the fight. Oaks folded up again, and then he just kept going and fell to the canvas, clutching his ribs. I wouldn't have been surprised if several of them were broken.

I looked over at Roy Wagner, who was shaking his head and writing in his notebook. I stole a glance at Maggie, and she was alternating between looking at Wagner and at Curry. Billy Harris was nowhere to be seen.

Dan Curry threw his son a towel as Don climbed out of the ring, but instead of congratulating him, old Dan tore into the boy. I guess Dan figured it took him too long to put Oaks away. Oaks was helped from the ring by Ben Neal and Bat, and then Bat went right to ring center to introduce the next two combatants.

The next four fights were either wild swinging affairs, or dance contests, and I could see the wisdom of Bat's match-ups there. Put the two swingers and the two dancers together and you'll have either a fairly interesting fight, or a long one. Put a dancer and a swinger together, and eventually the swinger will put the dancer away.

In any case, the crowds loved it when there were two men in the ring trying to decapitate each other, and only booed when the dancers got into the later rounds without damage to either fighter.

Whichever way you looked at it, it was an afternoon of entertainment.

"That's it, folks," Bat announced after the last bout. "Be back here tomorrow at the same time."

I watched the crowd drift away, for the most part satisfied that they'd gotten their money's worth, and the topic on everyone's mind seemed to be the way Don Curry punished Oaks.

"They're impressed with Curry," I said to Bat as he hopped down from the ring.

"He's got power, all right," Roy Wagner said from behind us.

"His old man wasn't satisfied," Bat said.

"His old man will never be satisfied," I said. I looked around for Maggie, but she was gone. I guess I had been a victim of becoming as interested in the bouts as everyone else.

"When does this other kid fight?" Wagner asked. "What did you say his name was? Harris?"

"Yeah, Billy Harris," Bat said. "He'll go in tomorrow's first bout."

"When does Curry go again?" Wagner asked.

"Day after tomorrow."

"When will they face each other?" Wagner asked.

Bat smiled an almost shy smile and said, "In the final, I guess."

"I see," Wagner said. "You wouldn't want them to meet in an earlier round and have one knock the other out of the contest."

"I think we owe it to the townspeople to put on as good a final as we can," Bat said.

"I can understand that," Wagner said.

Bat looked at me and I said, "So can I."

Bat smiled, vindicated.

"We did okay today, Clint," he said. "Let's go to the saloon. First drink's on me."

"Besides, we've got to give Ben Neal his money."

"Yeah, but we'll have to negotiate," Bat said. "I hadn't really intended him to work every fight."

"What happened?"

Bat laughed and said, "He told me I'd have to knock him down to get him out of the ring, and you know nobody's ever done that before."

THIRTY-SIX

At the saloon we grabbed the familiar corner table and Ben Neal brought us three beers, and one for himself.

"First round is on me," he insisted. "I can't tell you what it meant to me to be back in the ring like that. Clint, I want you and Bat to know how much I appreciated it."

"Yeah, so much that you threatened me when I tried to get you out of the ring," Bat said, kidding Ben good-naturedly.

"I'm sorry about that."

"Don't worry about it," Bat told him. "You did a better job than Clint or I could have done."

That was very true. With his experience in the ring, Ben knew just when to leave the fighters alone, and when to get in between them, something Bat and I could only guess at. Bat was right, we'd adjust the amount of money we were going to pay Ben and let him work all of the fights.

In fact, Bat got up and walked back to the bar with Ben to work it out, while I sat there with Roy Wagner.

"Roy," I said. "About those stories that Bat told you—the ones concerning the two of us and Wyatt Earp?"

"Yes?"

"I wouldn't print any of that if I was you."

"I've got Bat's permission," he said.

"In writing?" I asked, hoping that Bat had not been foolish enough to sign anything.

"Uh, no, not in writing," he admitted.

"Well, you don't have my permission, and you certainly don't have Wyatt Earp's permission."

"You mean that you and Earp would sue me?" he asked.

It was one of those rare times when I took advantage of my reputation.

"Wagner," I said, leaning towards him, "do you really think that men like Wyatt Earp and myself would bother to sue you?"

That gave him something to think about, and he was still thinking about it when Bat came back.

"All set?" I asked him.

"Yes," he said, giving Roy Wagner an odd look. "Ben and I worked it out. What, uh, happened here?"

"Here?" I said, and then looking at Wagner I said, "Roy and I just worked something out."

Wagner had one beer with us and then excused himself, saying that he had to do some writing.

When he was gone Bat looked at me and said, "What did you say to the man?"

I told him exactly what had gone on and then said, "I've only got one thing to say to you, Bat, and I hope you think about it: Be very careful before you sign your name to anything. That's it, the rest is up to you."

"Yeah, but the man just wants to—"

"Just think about it," I told him, standing up. "I'm going to see if I can find Maggie. I want to talk to her about what happened yesterday."

Leaving the saloon, I wondered why I hadn't thought to tell Bat that I saw Maggie and Roy Wagner talking together outside of town, and that since then Wagner had denied knowing either Maggie or her brother. Two questions then: Why hadn't I told Bat about it? Maybe because he and Wagner had become too friendly too fast. Bat was still young, and he still had a lot to learn about people.

The other question in my mind was why Roy Wagner had denied knowing Maggie and Billy Harris. And would Maggie deny knowing Wagner? That was what I wanted to find out.

I tried the livery area where Billy was training, and when I found neither one of them there, I headed for the boardinghouse. As I was approaching it, though, the front door opened and out stepped Roy Wagner. He didn't see me and I wanted to keep it that way, so I ducked behind a nearby buckboard and waited until he had gone past before I continued. Mrs. Halliday answered the door and answered a question in my mind at the same time.

"Oh my, two gentleman callers in the same day," she said when I asked for Maggie. I didn't comment, because it was enough for me to know that Wagner had indeed seen Maggie. Now I wanted to see what Maggie had to say.

"I'll call her down for you," Mrs. Halliday said.

"I would appreciate it, Mrs. Halliday, if you didn't tell her that I knew Mr. Wagner was here to see her."

The elderly lady smiled and said in a conspiratory whisper, "I understand, young man."

I was glad she thought she understood. There was a lot going on that I wished I understood. Maybe if I explained it all to Mrs. Halliday she'd be able to make me understand.

"I don't want to talk about yesterday," Maggie said glumly when she came down. She didn't look well at all. There was some darkness beneath her eyes and she looked haggard and tired.

"All right," I said. "We won't talk about it." She looked surprised. "We won't talk about it," I repeated. "I'll respect your wishes, because I'm not out to upset you. What did you think of today's fights?"

"I wasn't impressed," she said, still watching me warily, wondering why I wasn't pressing her about what Billy Harris had done to Jed Hunt.

"Not even with Don Curry?" I asked, watching her reaction closely.

"He didn't fight anybody," she said. "He fought a nobody and it still took him four rounds. Billy would have gone right to the body and finished that fella in the first round. Curry's not smart enough."

"He's powerful, though. He beat that fella with body punches."

"He's powerful, I admit," she said, "but he's not smart enough. Billy will do exactly what I tell him to do. With my brains and his speed, he'll beat anybody."

"You may be right."

"Is this what you came by to talk to me about?" she asked.

"Well, we could talk about the other night," I said, meaning the night we spent together.

"No, we can't talk about that," she said, stiffening. "That was a mistake."

This woman got stranger and stranger.

"All right, so we won't talk about that, either. Did you know that there's a newspaperman in town to cover these matches?"

"What?" she asked, obviously thrown off balance by the question—which was my intention.

"A newspaperman—"

"I heard you," she said, interrupting me. "No, I didn't know that."

"His name's Roy Wagner," I said, again watching her closely for her reaction.

"Wagner?"

"Yeah. He's from back East. Have you ever heard of him?"

"No, why should I?" she asked. "Just because he's from the East doesn't automatically mean I'm going to know him. No, I don't know him."

"Oh," I said. "All right. I just thought you might know him, or that you might want to know he was in town. He was at the fights today, and he'll probably be there tomorrow as well."

"Fine, let him be there," she said. "He'll see

a real fighter. Look, Clint I have to go and talk to Billy. Is that all you wanted?"

"Yes, Maggie," I said. "I think I got everything I wanted. Thanks."

"Sure."

She might have had to go and find Billy, but right at that moment she wasn't moving, so I turned around and walked out, leaving her standing in the middle of the room.

She had denied knowing Roy Wagner, even though only moments before he had been there talking to her.

Not only that, when I mentioned his name I thought I saw a flicker of fear cross her face.

Why would Maggie Harris, a woman who didn't scare easily, be afraid of Roy Wagner?

THIRTY-SEVEN

Billy Harris was very impressive. His opponent was more formidable—in size, anyway—than Don Curry's had been, but he dispatched him in two rounds less. Even with her brother in the ring, though, Maggie still couldn't keep from stealing glances at Roy Wagner. Still, after the fight she had a lot to say to Billy, and none of it looked good. He kept that look on his face of a child who has done something to displease his parent the whole time she was talking to him. I had been very impressed with his performance. He had stalked his opponent during the first round, effectively blocking the other man's punches and obviously looking for the quickest way to get to him. In round two, he went after his man, bulled his way through his meager defenses, and put him away with three vicious punches. Two body shots caused the man's hands to drop, and then a wicked right to the head knocked him out.

I had been very interested in seeing Billy Harris fight, especially after what he had done to Jed Hunt. This time, though, Billy had fought a very controlled fight, and that had impressed me even more than his power. Still, the other man had not laid a hand on him, and he hadn't gone after Jed Hunt until Jed hit him once. It still remained to be seen whether the next time he got hit, he'd react the same way.

During the second fight—a wild swinging affair—Maggie reappeared, probably wanting to check out the possible competition for Billy. Billy wasn't there, but then he didn't have to be, because Maggie took care of his fight tactics. I thought it might be a good time for me to find Billy and see what he had to say about Roy Wagner.

I worked my way through the crowd and walked back to town. Billy would probably go back to the boardinghouse to clean up, and then wait there for Maggie.

Mrs. Halliday once again let me in, but told me that Maggie wasn't in.

"I'm looking for Billy Harris, ma'am," I told her.

"Oh?" she said, looking slightly alarmed. I wondered what would bother her about my looking for Billy when she asked me, "Can you keep a secret?"

"What kind of a secret?"

"Well, Miss Harris takes good care of her brother, but the poor boy never seems to get enough to eat." She looked around, as if someone might be listening, and then she lowered her voice to a whisper and said, "He's in the kitchen, having a piece of my blueberry pie. You won't tell on him, will you?"

"I promise you, ma'am, not a word."

"I knew I could trust you," she said. "He's right through there," she added, pointing.

"Thank you, Mrs. Halliday." I started for the kitchen and from behind me she said, "Help yourself to a piece of pie, young man."

"Thank you."

Billy was sitting at the kitchen table devouring a large piece of pie. There was also a glass of milk in front of him. When he saw me he didn't look happy, either because I'd caught him eating a piece of pie, or for some other reason.

"Hello, Billy," I said, sitting opposite him.

"I don't want to talk to you," he said, sullenly.

"I thought we were friends."

"I don't want to talk to you," he said again, in the same tone, and he shoved a piece of pie into his mouth.

"Did Maggie tell you not to talk to me?" I asked.

"Maggie told me not to talk to anybody," he answered.

"But Maggie and I are friends," I said. "You can talk to me."

"You're not Maggie's friend," he said, accusingly. "You—" He stopped short and put another piece of pie into his mouth.

"What, Billy?" I asked. "I what?"

"You're not our friend," he said. "I don't want to talk to you. I don't like you."

"Why don't you like me?"

"Because of what you did," he said.

"What did I do?"

He hesitated a moment, then said, "You know."

What did he think I had done to her? Did it have to do with that night we'd spent together? What had she told him we had been doing?

"You're very protective of your sister, aren't you, Billy?" I asked.

He nodded.

"Do you love her?"

"Yes," he said.

"Would she be mad if she knew you were eating that piece of pie?"

He gave me a frightened look and said, "You won't tell her, will you?"

"Not if we're friends, Billy. A friend never tells on another friend."

"We can't be friends," he whined, looking down at his half-eaten pie.

"Finish the pie, Billy," I said. "I won't tell. I promise."

He looked at me as if trying to decide if I was telling the truth. In the end it was the allure of Mrs. Halliday's blueberry pie that made him decide I could.

"I would like you to answer one question for me, Billy," I said. "After that I won't bother you. Okay?"

He ignored me and drank some milk, then cut another chunk off his pie and put it in his mouth.

"Billy, do you know a newspaperman from back East named Roy Wagner?"

He was in the act of putting the last piece of pie in his mouth when I said Wagner's name, and I saw him stop momentarily, and then hurriedly put the piece away.

"You do, don't you?" I prompted.

"No," he said with his mouth full.

"Billy, it isn't nice to lie."

He looked stubborn and began to chew frantically.

"Billy—"

"I don't want to talk to you," he insisted. He finished his milk and stood up.

"Billy," I said, standing up also. "Why is your sister afraid of Roy Wagner?"

That stopped him. He looked at me real close and said, "Maggie ain't afraid of anybody. She's got me, and I won't let anybody touch her, or hurt her. I'd hurt anybody who hurt her, real bad," he added. From the look on his face, I believed him.

"As far as I know, nobody's hurt your sister, Billy," I said. "I haven't hurt her."

I put my hand on his arm and he pulled it away violently.

"I don't want to talk to you no more. I have to go upstairs and wait for Maggie."

"All right, Billy," I said.

He started for the door and then turned around and gave me a very solemn look.

"You won't tell Maggie about the pie?"

"I won't tell, Billy. I promise."

He gave me a smile like a big kid, and then walked out of the room.

At that point I realized that I'd had my hand on my gun. I wondered how long it had been there, and dropped my hand to my side.

THIRTY-EIGHT

By the time I got back the third fight was about to end. Both younger fighters were obviously too tired to stand up for very much longer, and finally one of them fell to the canvas and stayed there. Both men were helped from the ring, and Bat introduced the next two.

I looked for Maggie but she was gone. I didn't think much of it until I looked for Roy Wagner and found that he too had gone.

I worked my way through the crowd to Bat who was standing at ringside.

"Did you see Maggie?" I asked him.

"What?" He hadn't taken his eyes off the ring.

I grabbed his arm so he'd look at me and asked again, "Did you see Maggie?"

"She left."

"Alone?" He frowned at me and I said, "Did she leave with Roy Wagner?"

"No," he said, shaking his head.

"When did Wagner leave?"

He thought a moment and then said, "Right after she did, I think."

I let his arm go and he turned his attention back to the action—or lack of it—in the ring.

I decided to go and find Maggie, Roy Wagner, or both and find out what the story was. The problem was where to look. They couldn't have gone to the boardinghouse, because I had been there with Billy. Where else could they have gone?

I went back to my hotel and asked the desk clerk if Mr. Wagner had come in, either alone or with anybody.

"I didn't notice," he said in his bored way. That figured.

I went upstairs to Wagner's room and knocked. When there was no answer I tried to door knob and found the door unlocked. I went in.

I don't know what I expected to find—maybe the two of them in bed—but what I found was nothing.

I tried the saloon next, with no luck. I decided to check the livery stable and see if they were there, or if maybe they hadn't taken a couple of horses, or a buckboard.

Maybe they rode out of town for another private talk.

Walking through town I could hear the uproar caused by the fights. There must have been another good one going on, because the crowd was making an incredible racket, the kind they make when two men are trying to knock each other's head off.

When I entered the livery stable there was no one immediately in sight. Obviously, if anyone had any business to conduct, it would have to wait until after the fights were over.

I walked through the stable and out in back to check the corral. When I didn't find them there I decided to see if there was a buckboard missing, or a horse. While I was looking I looked in on Duke, intending to give him a few friendly words. I'd been neglecting him of late.

When Duke saw me he flared his nostril and tossed his head. Something was bothering him.

"What is it, big boy?" I asked, patting his neck. I had come to trust Duke's instinct without question over the years. He had saved my life more than once.

"Easy, pal," I said, patting his neck to calm him down. I looked around as far as I could see, and then gave him a last pat and left his stall. Something was bothering him, meaning something had happened inside that stable.

Or something was going to happen.

I eased my gun out of my holster and held it ready. I started checking the other stalls but found only horses. None were missing, I noticed. There were some empty stalls, but they had obviously been empty for some time.

Next I checked on the buckboards and buggies that were for rent. One of the buckboards had a tarp over the bed, so I held my gun up and grasped it with my free hand, then yanked it off hard and pointed my gun at . . . nothing.

I couldn't understand it. Duke had never been wrong before, and there was definitely something bothering him. I could still hear him snorting and pawing at the ground.

I had one place left to check, and that was the buggy. I walked around the buckboard and, with my gun ready, approached the buggy from behind. If there was anybody in that stable with me he must have been part Indian, because he hadn't made a sound that I could hear.

I put my back up against the back of the buggy and then started working around to the side so I could look inside. Sitting there as quiet as a corpse was Roy Wagner. And with good reason. The way his head lolled over to one side, I knew that his neck was broken. This wasn't anybody's idea of an "accident."

THIRTY-NINE

My first reaction was to go and find the sheriff, but then remembering what kind of lawman Sheriff Tyler was I decided that could wait. I took the tarp from the buckboard and covered Roy Wagner with it, then went to make sure Duke had calmed down.

"It's okay, big boy. It's okay," I told him, rubbing his big nose. He seemed to sense that I was in control of the situation, and he calmed down.

I left the livery and started walking towards all of the commotion that the fights were causing, wondering what the hell had happened.

Had Wagner left with Maggie, and if so, had Maggie killed him? Was she that strong? Billy was certainly strong enough to have done it, but the timing would have had to have been perfect.

Was Maggie's fear enough of a motive for me to suspect her of murder? And if she was afraid of Wagner, why? I was going to make a point of asking her, but first I had to get the body taken care of.

As I reached the crowd the last fight ended and the spectators started crowding out.

"Tomorrow, same time," I heard Bat yell, and the crowd cheered.

I approached the ring as Bat and Ben Neal hopped down.

"We did even better than yesterday," Bat told me.

"In some ways," I said.

"What do you mean?"

"I just found Roy Wagner," I told him, "in the livery stable with a broken neck."

"Jesus!" he said. "Dead?"

I nodded.

"Christ!" he said, rubbing his hand over his mouth. "What do we do?"

"Get the sheriff, I guess," I said. "Although what good he'll do I don't know."

"What about the mayor?" he asked.

"Yeah, him too."

Ben Neal was listening in and he said, "Who'd want to kill that writer fellow?"

"I've got some idea about that," I said, looking at Bat. "Ben, you better get back over to the saloon."

"Can I do anything—" he started to ask.

"Yes," I said, "don't mention this to anyone, all right? I'm trusting you."

"You can count on me, Clint," he said, and hurried off. I hoped he'd be able to keep his mouth shut at least for a little while.

"Was Maggie there?" Bat asked.

"No. Bat, did you notice the way Maggie kept watching him yesterday and today?"

He thought a moment then shrugged and said, "No, I can't say that I did. What's wrong?"

"I've been watching them," I said, and then explained why by telling him that I had seen them together outside of town. "They didn't look like strangers, either," I finished.

"Why didn't you tell me about that before?" he demanded.

"You were getting pretty chummy with Wagner," I said. "You wanted to tell him your life's story, remember?"

"But we're supposed to be partners, damn it!"

"Look, we'll fight about it later, okay? You go get the sheriff, I'll get the mayor, and I'll meet you at the livery."

"What about the undertaker?"

"Not yet. Get going."

We went in our separate directions. I had given him the task of getting the sheriff, because I didn't want to intimidate him any more than I had to.

Mayor Holman greeted my news with a horrified look and began to sputter something about closing down the tournament.

"Look, Mr. Mayor," I said. "Let's not start making empty threats, okay? We've been through this once before."

"What do we do?" he demanded. "Tyler can't handle this."

"I know that. I've decided to accept the offer you made to me last time we spoke. I'll work for you."

"We can't pay much—"

"That's the least of your worries. There's a

killer loose in this town, and I don't want a panic to spread. I don't want the townspeople to panic, and I don't want the killer to panic. Come with me to the livery stable."

"To see the body?" he asked, looking horrified again. "Do you really need me—"

"Mr. Mayor, he's dead. He's not going to bite you. I need you to tell that fool Tyler that I'm in charge, and that I want it to be our little secret. Let's go."

I damn near dragged him to the door and he finally got his legs under him and walked with me.

Bat and Tyler were already there, looking at the body.

"Must have been somebody strong," Tyler was saying as we entered. He heard us come in and turned, and when he saw me he froze up.

"Jesus," I said under my breath, but aloud I said, "Good observation, sheriff."

"Mr. Mayor," Tyler said, frowning at both of us.

"Would you tell the sheriff about our arrangement, Mr. Mayor?" I said to Holman.

He explained to Tyler that I was to be in charge of investigating this terrible crime, and that Tyler was to help me in any way he could.

"Does that mean he's sheriff?" Tyler asked.

"No, you're still sheriff," I said, answering before the mayor could. "I'm not concerned with keeping law and order in your town, except where it concerns this murder, and the other incidents."

"Do you think Dell Curry was also killed on purpose?" Bat asked.

"This was obviously no accident," I said, "and I think we have to assume that Dell's death wasn't, either."

"What could they have in common?" Bat asked. "Wagner wasn't even in town when Dell was killed."

"I know," I said, "but there's a connection, not only between these two killings, but the other accidents, as well."

"Do you think someone wants to kill my boy?" the mayor asked.

"No, Mr. Mayor. I think what happened to those three men was just what was supposed to happen. I don't think those men are in any danger."

The mayor looked relieved.

"Sheriff, why don't you go over and get the undertaker, and then you and he can carry the body to his office."

"People are gonna ask questions," he said.

"Just tell them that it was another accident, and that you have everything under control."

Tyler threw the mayor a dirty look, and then went off to do what I told him.

"I hope he keeps his mouth shut," Bat said.

"He will if he values his job," the mayor said. "Do you still need me?"

"No, you can go—and please keep this quiet."

He looked offended that I would even remind him, but said nothing and hurried away.

"What a pair," Bat said.

"Yeah."

"What do you think?"

· "I don't know what to think, Bat," I said. "I have to talk to Maggie."

"What about the kid?"

"The kid?" I said, looking at him. "I think that 'kid' scares the hell out of me, Bat."

FORTY

We waited until Tyler and the undertaker returned, and then left the body in their hands.

"Damn," Bat said as we were leaving the stable.

"What?"

"I've got to take care of today's receipts," he said.

"Okay, go ahead. This is my problem anyway, remember? I'm security."

"Just let me know what I can do," he said.

"I will."

We split up, and I headed for the boarding-house. Mrs. Halliday answered and I was probably a little impatient with her when I asked for Maggie.

"I'll get her," she said.

"I'd like to go up myself, ma'am. Which room is it?"

"Oh dear," she said. "I don't think—"

I didn't wait for her to tell me what she thought. I started up the stairs and she called out, "Second door to the right," probably so I wouldn't bust in on one of her other boarders.

I walked to the door and knocked, calling out, "Maggie!"

When she didn't answer I yelled, "Maggie, it's Clint. Open the door."

She swung her door open angrily and said, "What do you think you're—"

I pushed past her and said, "Close the door."

"I will not!" she snapped. I reached back and slammed the door shut, yanking it from her hand.

"Are you crazy?" she demanded, glaring at me.

"I want to know about you and Roy Wagner," I said.

"What—"

"Maggie, I saw you outside of town the other day, and you weren't talking like strangers who had just met. Why were you so afraid of him?"

"I wasn't—"

"Listen to me!" I said, grabbing her by the elbows. "He's dead, the man is dead, and you are damn high on my list of people who might have killed him."

"What?" she said, shocked. "He's dead? How—"

"Somebody real strong snapped his neck for him," I said.

I let go of her elbows and she staggered back a few steps. She looked so shocked that I really believed that she hadn't known anything about it.

"Maggie—"

"Wait a minute, wait a minute!" she snapped, pressing her fists to her temples. "I have to be able to think. Give me a chance to think."

I backed off a bit. Pressing her wasn't going to help.

"Billy," she said, finally, "where's Billy?"

"I don't know—" I said, but before I could say more she'd opened the door and run out down the hall. I followed, and found her one door down, pounding on it and calling Billy's name.

"He doesn't answer," she said.

"Step back," I told her. I braced myself against the opposite wall and then kicked at the door. It swung open with a loud bang, and Maggie rushed in.

"He's not here," she said when I entered behind her. "We have to find him."

"Maggie, why—"

"I'll explain, Clint, but we have to find him."

"Come on," I said, grabbing her arm.

We rushed downstairs where Mrs. Halliday was waiting.

"What in heavens name—" she started, but we didn't give her a chance to continue.

"Mrs. Halliday, it's very important that we find Billy Harris. Do you know where he is?"

"No," she said. "I saw him leave, but I don't know where he went."

"Was he alone?" Maggie asked.

The elderly woman sniffed and said, "I should say he wasn't alone." It was more than plain that she strongly disapproved of whoever it was Billy had left with.

"Well, who was he with?" I prompted her.

"A nice boy like that—"

"Mrs. Halliday!" I snapped.

"I'm sorry, Miss Harris," she told Maggie, "but your brother left with the town trollop—"

"Who, Mrs. Halliday?" I asked.

"—and her father so prim and proper, and he knows what she's been up to. No better than a common whore, and a doctor's daughter."

"Melody Gilman?" I asked in surprise.

"Of course, who did you think? She's had her eye on that boy since he got to town—"

Maggie and I didn't hear the rest, because we had already run outside. Maggie's panic was becoming infectious, and I began to fear for Melody Gilman's safety.

FORTY-ONE

"Anything?" I asked Bat as he entered the saloon.

"No, nothing. We've checked the town twice, and we can't find a trace of either of them."

He sat down, pulled my drink over to him and downed it.

It was several hours after Maggie and I had left the boardinghouse, and we had organized a small, select search party to look for Billy Harris and Melody Gilman. The search party consisted of Maggie and myself, looking together; Bat and his Bonnie Mapes—whom I had finally met and sworn to secrecy; Sheriff Tyler, Mayor Holman, and his boy, Bob Holman. We had also recruited Iron Ben Neal who, to my surprise had actually kept his mouth shut about Wagner's death.

One by one the others trickled in and also reported having found nothing. Bat had sent Bonnie off to bed, but the rest of us were eventually seated around a table in the saloon, which we had closed early. That turned out to be no problem because—no surprise—it turned out to be owned by Mr. Mayor himself.

"What about her father?" I asked.

"The good doctor?" Sheriff Tyler asked. "He won't talk to anybody about his sweet little girl."

As it turned out, I had indeed been fooled by the seemingly sweet and shy Melody Gilman who, it turned out, was well-known for her round heels.

"He won't admit to himself that his daughter's a free whore," Tyler said.

"What man would?" I asked. "I guess I'll have to go over and talk to him. Maggie?"

"I'll come," she said.

We both stood up and I looked at the others and said, "Keep looking."

"Where?" Bat asked.

"All the same places," I said. "And Bat—everybody—don't hurt him if you can avoid it."

That was for Maggie's benefit. I knew none of them was going to take a chance on having their necks broken, and Maggie probably knew it, too.

As we walked towards the doctor's place I said, "You want to explain now?"

"There's a lot to tell," she said. "Clint, if that girl tries to seduce Billy, I—I don't know what he'd do."

"He killed Dell Curry, didn't he?" I asked her. "Because of what happened in the alley that day?"

She looked at me with anguished eyes and nodded.

"Jesus, does he know about us?" I asked.

"I didn't tell him, but I think he knows," she said.

That explained why he didn't want to talk to me, why he said I wasn't their friend because of what I had *done* to Maggie.

"And he killed Roy Wagner?"

"I—I think so," she said, her voice breaking. "Oh, Clint, I don't even know for sure that he killed Dell, but—"

"But you feel that he did?"

She nodded.

"Maggie, has something like this happened before?" I asked.

"Y-yes."

"Back East?"

"Yes."

It was all falling into place now.

"And Roy Wagner knew about it?"

"Yes. Billy got into some trouble, over a girl . . ."

"Was she killed?"

"No," she said, quickly, "but she was beaten up. Oh, she was asking for it. She was like this girl, always trying to get into anyone's pants, but her father was an important man—" She stopped and put her hand over her mouth for a moment, then continued. "We left town and I changed our names, but there wasn't any other way we could make money but to have Billy fight."

"Wagner followed?"

"Yes. He wanted a story, he wanted me," she said. "Maybe he didn't even know what he really wanted. He found out we were here and sent me a telegram, for God's sake. I replied and arranged to meet him outside of town, to try and persuade him to leave, or at least keep quiet until after Billy fought McCoole."

"What did he say?"

"He said he'd see. He said it depended on how I treated him."

"What happened in the stable?"

"We left the fights together. He said he wanted to talk to me alone. When we got to the stable he tried to force himself on me. He had me down on the ground . . . my shirt was torn . . . Billy came in. He was looking for me after you talked to him, and when he saw Roy Wagner on top of me he just . . . went crazy. He picked him up from behind and he just . . . just . . ."

He just snapped Wagner's neck like a dry twig. When was he going to come after me, I wondered?

"What about the accidents to those three men?" I asked.

"I don't know," she said. "I honestly don't know."

"Had any of them approached you?"

"No, none of them. I had little or no contact with any of them."

So there were still some things to be explained . . . and there was still Billy to find, and Melody Gilman—alive, hopefully.

We got to the doctor's rooms and climbed the stairway. I knocked on the door and his deep voice called out, "Go away."

"Open up, doctor," I shouted. "Don't make me kick the door in."

I pushed Maggie off to one side, in case he had a

gun and started firing through the door, but it proved an unnecessary precaution. I heard the lock on the door and then it swung open.

"Come in, then," he said.

I went in first and Maggie behind me. The man looked much older than the last time I'd seen him, and he looked sick.

"Doctor, we have to find your daughter," I said.

He shook his head and large tears started falling down his face.

"I tried the best I could after her mother . . . was killed . . . but I couldn't control her. She could twist men . . . around her little fingers. . . . You know," he said, looking at me. He put his hand over his face and said, "God forgive me, she even did it to me. I couldn't help it. She's so soft, so lovely . . . the image of her mother . . ."

I found myself disgusted by the thought that he had been seduced by his own daughter, and I could see that Maggie felt the same.

"Doctor, please," I said, not wanting to hear anymore of that. "Whatever she is, we've got to find her before something happens to her."

"Whatever she is," he repeated. "A slut, a whore. I've refused to admit until now—"

"Doctor, for God's sake, she doesn't deserve to die," I said. "She's gone off with a very disturbed young man. We've got to find them, for both their sakes."

"Perhaps she will finally get what she deserves," he said, but he wasn't speaking to us. I was about to try again when I heard someone coming up the stairs outside.

"Clint!" Bat's voice called.

I opened the door and found Bat standing outside, alone.

"Did you find them?" I asked.

"We found her," he said, looking past me at Maggie and the girl's father.

"Where, Bat?"

"The Currys just brought her in," he said. I looked at him and he nodded and said, "She's dead."

I heard Maggie's sharp intake of breath, and I heard the doctor say something that sounded like "Thank God."

FORTY-TWO

Everyone was gathered around the front of the hotel, and the body of Melody Gilman was slung unceremoniously over the back of a horse. Doctor Gilman had remained behind, which was all right with me.

"Okay, settle down," I called out. All faces turned towards me, Dan Curry's carrying its usual portion of hatred.

"I understand you're in charge here," he said.

"That's right."

He pulled a blanket off of the body and showed it to us.

"Broken neck?" I asked.

"Looks like," Dan Curry said.

"Where'd you find her, Dan?" I asked.

"Oh, you mean you don't think we killed her?" he asked.

"You wouldn't come riding into town with her if you had. I give you credit for more brains than that. Where did you find her?"

"The boys found her in the barn out by our camp."

"Have you been using the barn?"

"Not that one," he said. "There's a newer one closer to the house that we use. This one is farther back, behind the house."

"We noticed that the door was open," Don spoke up. "Me and Dave went to check it out, and we found her."

"Did you know who she was?" I asked.

"Hell, yes," Old Dan said. "I chased this slut away from the ranch more than once. She was on the lookout for trouble, this one."

I noticed both boys looking anywhere else but at their pa, and figured that Melody had caught one or both of them, in spite of Dan's attempts to chase her away.

"I get the feeling you know who did this," Dan said.

"I've got an idea," I said. I directed myself to Don and Dave. "Did you boys see anyone else by that barn?"

"No, not a soul."

"Did you check out the barn completely?"

They looked at each other and Dave said, "No, we didn't. We picked the girl up and carried her out."

"Sheriff, why don't you go with them over to the undertaker's office."

"Yeah," he said, sullenly. "This way," he told them and they followed. Then Dan turned and looked at me.

"The same person who killed her kill my boy Dell?" he asked.

"I think so, Dan."

He hesitated, then said, "I guess you didn't kill him, then."

"No, I guess I didn't," I replied. "And I guess you Currys didn't have anything to do with those accidents."

He nodded, started off, then turned again and said, "I still owe you, Adams."

"I understand," I told him, and he hurried after his boys and the sheriff.

"What now?" Bat asked.

"I think you should send these people home," I told him, then took Maggie's arm and took her inside. A few minutes later, Bat and Ben Neal came in, also.

"He's got to be in that barn," I said to the three of them.

"Why?"

"Because those boys carried the girl out and never checked the rest of it. If he's in there, he probably figures nobody'll look there now." I looked at Maggie and said, "Could he reason that out that way?"

"I think so. He's like a little boy—"

"—and little boys have been known to be pretty tricky," I finished. "Bat, let's get out there."

"I want to come."

"Stay here, Maggie," I said, firmly. "Just stay here. We'll bring him back."

I looked at Bat and we went out to get our horses. I fully intended to try and bring Billy Harris in alive, but if it was necessary to . . . subdue him forcibly, I didn't want her to be there.

FORTY-THREE

During the ride out there I made sure that Bat knew I wanted to take Billy Harris alive.

"If he lets us, fine," Bat said. "But I'm not going to get my neck broken just so you can do it."

"I don't expect you to," I said. "Just don't be quick on the trigger."

"Okay," he said. "Damn, do you know what this does to the tournament?"

"Yes, I do. It makes Don Curry the sure winner, and he'll fight Mike McCoole. What's wrong with that?"

"Ah, I wanted to have a real good final between Harris and Curry."

"Maybe one of the other fellas will surprise you," I said.

"Sure."

That was all of the conversation that took place. The rest of the ride was made in silence.

"Let's leave the horses here," I suggested as we approached the barn. We dismounted, and he tied his horse off. As always, I left Duke free, knowing that he wasn't going anywhere.

"Let's be as quiet as we can be, all right?" I suggested.

"Okay. This is your play, Clint. I'll back you."

I nodded, and led the way.

Night had fallen and the moon was full by now. We could see the old barn even from twenty or thirty yards off. It wasn't very large. The Curry boys could have stumbled on him very easily if indeed he was inside when they found Melody, and then Bat's "final" would have taken place right there and then.

I stopped Bat and said, "Why don't you let me go in alone first?"

"Do you think that's the way to play it?" he asked.

"Maybe we can avoid trouble if I go in and talk to him," I suggested.

He thought it over a moment, then said, "All right, but I'll stay close by so I can come in at the first sign of trouble."

I gave him a light punch on the arm and said, "Good enough. Come on."

We moved forward quietly and when we reached the front door Bat backed off and tried the door. The Currys had closed it behind them, but it was unlocked and opened easily. It was old, though, and creaked as it opened, effectively announcing my arrival.

It was dark inside and I left the door open so some of the moonlight would filter in—and so that Bat would be able to hear clearly what was going on inside.

"Billy," I called out, standing still while I

waited for my eyes to adjust to the dimness inside. "Billy Harris, I know you're in here."

Still no answer.

"Damn it, Billy, Maggie's worried about you."

I thought I heard someone take a deep breath, and then Billy's voice said, "Close the door."

I took a step back and swung the door closed. After a moment I heard the scratch of a match and then Billy lit a lamp and stepped forward.

He looked a mess. Dirty, sweaty . . . scared.

"Billy—"

"Where's Maggie?" he asked.

"She's waiting in town for you."

"She wants me to go back with you?"

"Yes."

"You're a liar," he said.

"No, I'm not, Billy."

"Yes, you are. You're not my friend, and you're not Maggie's friend. You're just like the others."

"What others?"

"Others who wanted to . . . touch Maggie."

"Like Dell Curry?"

"Yes, like him. He shouldn't have tried to hurt Maggie, to touch her. He paid for it."

"You killed him?"

"Yes."

"What about the other three, Billy?" I asked. "The three accidents. Did you do that, too?"

He lowered his eyes and said, "Yes, but that was different."

"Different? How?"

"I-I hurt them for their own good," he said.

"What do you mean, Billy?"

"I didn't want to have to hurt them in the ring. I thought if I fixed it so they couldn't fight, I wouldn't have to hurt them in the ring. I thought maybe some of the other men would pull out, and I wouldn't have to hurt them, either."

I guess there was some kind of logic behind that. What was illogical was that he was so concerned about not hurting people, and he had killed three people.

"Roy Wagner was a bad man," Billy said then. He looked up at me and said, "I'm glad I killed him. He's been hurting Maggie for a long time, but she wouldn't let me hurt him. Well, now he's dead."

"What about the girl, Billy?"

"Her!" he said, with distaste. "She wanted to—to do things with me. Bad things. The kind of things that men wanted to do with Maggie." Then he looked right at me and said, "The kind of things you *did* do with Maggie."

"Did Maggie tell you that, Billy?"

"She didn't have to," he said. "I'm not as dumb as everyone thinks I am. I knew where she was that night. I knew she was with you." He looked as if he were very proud of his cleverness.

"So what about me, Billy? Are you going to kill me, too?"

"Maggie didn't want me to hurt you," he said.

"Maggie sent me to get you."

"No, she didn't."

"Yes, she did."

He shook his head.

"Maggie said that we both had to stay away from you. She wouldn't send you out here to get me." He stiffened for a moment, then the look on his face changed. "You came out here to hurt me, didn't you? Who told you I was out here?"

I decided to try a new tack.

"The girl told us, Billy. Melody told us."

"No, no," he said. "She's dead. I killed her. I broke her neck."

"No, she's alive," I said. "She told me you were out here."

"You're trying to confuse me," he said.

"Billy—" I said, putting my hands in front of me, which was a mistake. I was trying to win his confidence, but he moved incredibly fast for a big man. He stepped towards me with a boxer's grace and hit me with his right hand. As I went down I tried to get my gun out, but he was on top of me. He drove a punch into my ribs which just about paralyzed me, and then he plucked my gun from my holster and threw it into the hayloft.

At that point the door creaked open and Billy moved towards it. As Bat entered with his gun held ahead of him, Billy grabbed the wrist of his gun hand with his left hand and hit him with a vicious right that I thought would tear his head off. Bat went down, and Billy came up with his gun and threw it into the hayloft, also.

Little by little the air started to work its way back into my lungs and I was able to move.

Billy closed the door and then rolled Bat away from it. He looked up and saw me looking at him.

"He's all right," he assured me. "I don't want to kill him. I don't have anything against him."

I struggled to my feet, holding onto my ribs, and said, "But you've got something against me, don't you, Billy."

"Yes," he said. "I want to hurt you."

"Did you want to hurt Jed Hunt?" I asked.

"Who?"

I wanted to keep him talking until I could get my breath back.

"The big man you hurt while you were sparring with him," I reminded him.

"Oh, him," he said. "I'm sorry about that. I didn't want to hurt him, I wanted to hurt you, but Maggie wouldn't let me go near you."

"So you took it out on him?"

"I said I was sorry about that," he said. "But now I have to kill you, and then Maggie and I will leave."

"Billy—"

The look on his face told me that there would be no use in talking to him. He started to move in on me and all I had to defend myself with was my bare hands . . . against a professional boxer who wanted to kill me.

"You going to break my neck, Billy?"

"I'm going to show you how it feels for a man to die in the ring," he told me.

Jesus Christ, I thought, he's going to beat me to death, and how could I hope to stop him?

FORTY-FOUR

He never looked bigger, or more dangerous, than he did bearing down on me with his fists balled up. They looked more deadly to me in that moment than any gun I had ever faced. I was always reasonably sure that I could defend myself from any man's gun.

This was different. This man—a man with a child's mind—who made his living with his fists, was intent on killing me with his hands, and I wasn't at all sure I could stop him, or even give him any kind of resistance.

"Billy, Maggie doesn't want you to kill anyone else," I said.

"I don't want to talk to you," he said.

I backed up until I couldn't back up anymore, and then as he rushed me I put up my hands to defend myself as best I could.

He threw a right that went through my guard and caught me flush on the chin. It drove my head back and I hit it on the inside wall. As I started to slide to the floor, he hit me in the stomach with his left and I saw spots of light before my eyes.

"Billy!" I heard someone shout.

It was Maggie.

He turned away from me and I lay there on the ground, with my cheek in the dirt. I could see Maggie standing by the door, and next to her was Ben Neal. She must have gotten Ben to bring her out there.

"Maggie?" Billy said, sounding puzzled.

"Billy, that's enough," she said. "Leave him alone."

"I have to kill him," he told her, and turned back to me.

"You have to stop him," Ben Neal told Maggie.

Tears streaming from her eyes, she said, "I don't think I can."

Billy bent over and grabbed me by the shirt. He hauled me to my feet and, over his shoulder, I could see little Iron Ben Neal rush forward, fists ready.

"Ben—" I said, but there was no warning him away. He threw a right that caught Billy in the middle of the back, causing his grip on me to loosen. I staggered back and braced myself against the wall to keep myself from falling.

Billy swung around towards Ben Neal, and they looked ludicrous facing each other. Billy was a good foot taller and eighty pounds heavier, but Ben had one thing going for him that I didn't, and that was that he had once fought professionally in the ring.

"I don't want to hurt you," Billy said.

"Bigger men have tried, friend," Ben told him, cockily.

"Ben," I croaked, "he'll kill you."

"Get out of here, Clint," Ben said, but Billy moved around in front of me. I wanted to throw myself at him, but I couldn't seem to find the strength to even crawl away from the wall.

I just stood there and helplessly watched as Ben Neal moved in on Billy Harris, holding his fists up. Billy drew his right hand back and launched a murderous right hand that caught Ben right on the chin. I couldn't believe it when Ben's head jerked back, but he didn't fall. The little man had taken Billy's best shot and he was still standing. Billy couldn't believe it, either, and Ben took advantage of the big man's surprise. He stepped in and drove one, two, three rights hands into Billy's midsection.

If anything, Ben's punches had even less effect on Billy than the boy's had on him. Billy grunted and retaliated by throwing a left that caught Ben in the ribs. The little man backed away hastily, but still did not fall.

"You can't knock me down," Ben told Billy. "Give it up."

Billy didn't answer, but it appeared that he had forgotten about me and was now concentrating solely on Ben.

They closed on each other and began to exchange vicious punches. Billy's were the heavier blows, but it looked to me like Ben was better able to take the punishment. Before long they were both bleeding, and Maggie was shouting at them to stop, but neither of them seemed to hear her.

They continued to exchange blows, and

unbelievably, Ben Neal seemed to be wearing the larger man down. For what seemed like hours, neither man had taken a backward step and now, unbelievably, for the first time, Billy Harris seemed to be moving back. He was giving way before Ben's attack. Then the old fighter threw two hard rights into Billy's midsection that caused the boy to drop his hands. At that point, Ben began to pepper Billy's face with rights and lefts. Then, suddenly, Ben stepped back out of his way. Billy hit the ground face down and didn't move, and Maggie rushed to her fallen brother.

Using the wall, I managed to stand up straight and the air began to come to my lungs a little easier.

Ben Neal, his face torn and bleeding, turned to me with a wide smile on his face and said, "Son-of-a-bitch! That's my first knock-out!"

And then he, too, fell.

EPILOGUE

We decided later that Iron Ben Neal's record was still intact, because it wasn't until after Billy Harris had been knocked out that Ben fell.

A few days later, Don Curry officially became the winner of the tournament by knocking his opponent out—and out of the ring—in the first round. All that remained after that was to await the arrival of the heavyweight champion, Mike McCoole.

Billy Harris was in Sheriff Tyler's jail, and it would be up to a court to decide his fate.

"What will you do, Maggie?" I asked her on my last day in town.

We were at the boardinghouse where I had gone to say goodbye.

"I'll do what I've always done, Clint," she answered. "I'll stay with him, and take care of him."

"I knew you would." I took her hands in mine and said, "Good luck, to both of you."

I left and went over to the saloon, where Bat and Ben Neal were having a drink. Ben's face was still a mess, but he wore the bruises and cuts proudly.

"What are you two talking about?" I asked, as I sat down with them.

"Ben here is considering challenging Don Curry for the right to meet Mike McCoole."

"I'm in shape," Ben said, putting up his fists.

"Ben," I said, putting my hand on his shoulder. "I owe you my life, but be satisfied with what you've got. Stay behind the bar."

"Naw, I'm through tending bar," Ben said. "Don't worry, I ain't gonna go back to fighting, but I am going back into the ring—as a referee!"

"Good for you," I said.

"And what are you going to do, pard?" Bat asked.

"I'm going to get moving," I told him. "I've been in one place for too long."

"What about the championship fight with McCoole?" Bat asked. "You're not going to stick around to see that?"

"I've had enough of the fight game for a while," I said.

"What about your share of the profits from the McCoole fight?" Bat asked.

"I'll take what I've got now and be on my way, Bat," I said. "Give my share of the McCoole money to Ben, here," I added, in a sudden inspiration.

We had already divvied up the proceeds from the tournament, so I stood up and extended my hand to Bat.

"I'll catch you somewhere down the road, Bat," I said as we shook hands.

"Thanks for the help, Clint," he said. "Without you, maybe the whole thing would have gone up in smoke."

"Bat," I said, making for the door, "that might not have been such a bad idea."